Etheldreda the Ready

Mrs. George de Horne Vaizey

Etheldreda The Ready

Chapter One

The first part of the Christmas holidays had gone with a roar. The Saxon family in conclave agreed that never before had they had so good a time. Invitations poured in; amusement after amusement filled up afternoon and evening; parents and friends alike seemed imbued with a wholly admirable desire to make the season one gay whirl of enjoyment, and then, suddenly, just after the beginning of the New Year, the atmosphere became mysteriously clouded.

What was the matter? Nobody knew. One day the sky was blue and serene—the next, the shadow was in possession. Mr Saxon looked suddenly old and bleached, and hid himself persistently in his study; Mrs Saxon sat at the head of the table with the air of one braced to perform a difficult task, listened vacantly to her children's prattle, and smiled a twisted smile in response to their merry outbursts of laughter. Two days later Miss Bruce, the governess, was summoned hastily to return from her holiday-making and take charge of the household, while Mr and Mrs Saxon set forth to pay a mysterious visit to their country house, which as a rule was left severely to the caretaker's mercies until spring was well advanced.

What in the world could have induced two people who were obviously worried and depressed to leave town and go down to that dull, deserted house in the depth of the winter? The Saxons discussed the subject with their wonted vivacity, and from the many divergent points of view with which they were accustomed to regard the world in general.

They were six in all, and as true Saxons in appearance as they were in name, being large, fair, flaxen-haired creatures, of the type which is unfortunately growing rarer year by year.

Rowena, tall and stately, had already reached the stage when womanhood and girlhood meet, but her undeniable beauty was somewhat marred by an air of self-consciousness, which was in truth more than half due to a natural shyness and diffidence in adapting herself to new conditions. Hereward, the Sandhurst cadet, and Gurth, the Eton stripling, were as handsome a pair as one could wish to meet. Etheldreda, with her flowing golden locks, widely open grey eyes and alert, vivacious features, might have sat as a type of a bonnie English schoolgirl, while the twins, Harold and Maud, were plump, pleasant-looking creatures, devoted to each other, who in holiday time could be turned into convenient fags for their elders and betters. Good old Harold could always be depended upon to do his duty with resignation, if not cheerfulness, but Maud was one of those constitutionally stupid people who are nevertheless gifted with sudden flashes of sharpness apt to prove embarrassing to their companions. The Saxons, to use their own expressive parlance, were always "a trifle wary" in dealing with Maud, for what that young lady thought she promptly *said*, and said without reserve, choosing, as it seemed, out of pure "cussedness" the very moment of all others when they would have had her silent.

Discussions and guesses alike failed to suggest any reasonable explanations of Mr and Mrs Saxon's mysterious behaviour, and Miss Bruce steadily refused to be drawn, though there was a certain something in her manner which convinced her charges that she was in the secret.

And then on the morning of the fifth day the blow fell, in the shape of a short, decisive note ordering the young people to pack their belongings and repair down to "The Meads" for the remainder of the holidays. The mandate was so firm and decisive that there was no hope of escape. The girls might cry and the boys might storm, but both realised the uselessness of protest. Assisted by Miss Bruce and Nannie, once nurse and now schoolroom maid, the melancholy preparations were made in time to allow the party to catch the three o'clock train from Victoria.

To secure a carriage in which they could travel alone and be able to talk as they pleased was the ambition of the four elders, and while Miss Bruce was busily looking after the luggage, they took possession of a corridor coupé, slammed the door, and blocked the window with determined faces, though deep in each heart lurked the conviction that Miss Bruce's morbidly acute conscience would feel it her duty to interfere.

"Nix for the Spider!" hissed Gurth, prising a hockey-stick against the handle of the door the while he gazed with elaborate calm at a poster on the station wall. It was inevitable that a person named Bruce should be given the nickname of "Spider" by young people who disdained correct appellations as heartily as did the Saxons, and, indeed, the busy little black figure darting to and fro on the platform might have been much less aptly named. She hustled the twins and Nannie into a carriage, turned her head to look for her elder pupils, and, upon realising the position, reared her head with the fighting gesture which they knew so well. For a moment, as she stood facing the coupé window, it seemed absolutely certain that she would insist upon joining the party, and so spoiling sport for the whole of the journey, but even as she looked her expression altered, a flicker of something—what was it?—affection, sympathy, pity passed over her face, she turned without a word, entered the carriage wherein the twins were seated, and disappeared from sight.

The plot had succeeded, but their success had left the conspirators dumb with wonder and surprise.

"I say! what's taken her all of a sudden?" ejaculated Gurth. Hereward whistled loudly, while Dreda, ever the prey of her emotions, began to flush and quiver beneath the prickings of remorse.

"Oh, poor dear! Oh, she *saw*! She saw we didn't want her! What brutes we are! Gurth, go!—go quickly, before the train starts, and tell her to come in here at once!"

"Not I! What a turncoat you are, Dreda! Of course she saw! We *meant* her to see. You were the worst of the lot, scowling as if she were an ogre. Don't be a little sneak!"

"Not a sneak!" protested Dreda, hotly. "S'pose I did. I can be sorry, can't I? She looked so—*sick*! It made me feel mean."

"All right! Go in to the other carriage, then, and suck up! We don't want her here, but there's room for you in there, if you like to change! Say the word! We are off in a minute!"

Etheldreda blushed, shuffled, and tossed her pigtail, but made not the slightest attempt to move from her place, whereat her brothers and sister chuckled with easy amusement.

> "Oh, Dreda, in our hours of ease,
>
> Uncertain, coy, and hard to please,
>
> And variable as the shade

4

By the light thingummy aspen made.

When pain and anguish wring the brow,

She nothing does, but makes a row."

The mutilated lines were the contributions of the two schoolboys, while Rowena looked down her nose once more, and dismissed the subject in a few scathing remarks.

"You might realise by this time that Dreda's sentiments have not the smallest influence on her actions! The Spider was evidently suffering from a spasm of repentance. Quite time, too! She has made herself most objectionable the last few days, sighing and groaning about the house, and looking as if her heart were broken. If *we* can stand breaking our engagements and giving up all the fun of the holidays, I don't see why she need grumble. But she is always like that—unsympathetic and absorbed in herself. It's a mystery to me, for what has she got to be absorbed in? To be old, and ugly, and poor, and to have no home or any people that count— there can't possibly be any personal interest in life! Her only hope would be to live for others, and of that, poor dear, she is incapable!"

Rowena folded her hands on her lap, turned her well-cut profile to the window, and sighed in an elderly, forbearing fashion, at which the two boys grinned broadly, while impetuous Dreda burst once more into speech.

"Rowena, I *hate* you when you talk like that! Don't be so self-righteous and horrid! It's not for you to criticise other people. The Spider is not a patch on you for selfishness, and if she has a poor time of it, that's all the more reason why you should be charitable, and try to cheer her up. You'll be old yourself some day, and ugly too! Fair people always fade soonest. I read that in the toilette column of a magazine, so it's true, and I shouldn't wonder if you grew nut-crackery, too. Your nose is rather beaky even now. You needn't be so proud!"

Rowena turned her head to look round the carriage with a gently tolerant smile.

"Our dear Dreda teaches us a lesson in charity, does she not?" she demanded blandly. That was all the response she deigned to make, but it was enough to reduce her sister to a crimson confusion, and to rouse Gurth to impatient anger.

"Oh, leave off nagging, you two!" he cried loudly. "If you don't drop it, I'll be off into a smoker at the first stop. Fight it out to-night when you are alone, if you can't agree; but let us off when we are caged up in the same pen. Here! Let's have a game of 'Roadside cribbage.' Bags I the left side! Now then, Dreda, I choose you first. Hereward can take Rowena. Buck up! We have got to win this time."

Etheldreda shot a glance of gratitude from the grey eyes which were such eloquent exponents of her thoughts. To be so championed by Gurth was worth far more than the temporary suffering inflicted by Rowena's sharp tongue, and she set herself valiantly to be worthy of his choice. "Roadside cribbage" was a game patronised for years by the Saxon family on their railway journeys, and consisted merely in dividing forces, staring steadily out of opposite windows, and scoring for the various objects perceived, according to a quaint but well understood method. Thus, a bridge over a river counted as five marks; a quarry, ten; a windmill, twenty; a fire, fifty; a motor car, minus one; while the ubiquitous bicycle was worth only three per dozen. These, and other objects too numerous to repeat, mounted but slowly towards the grand total of a hundred, but there remained one—just one rare chance of winning success at a stroke, for the competitor who had the luck to spy a cat looking out of a window might cry, "Game!" on the instant, even if he had not so far scored a single point. It can easily be understood that the best chances of spotting this valuable spectacle came as the train slackened steam before entering a station. Then, as one regarded the backs of dreary tenement houses, it really seemed inevitable that some household cat should wish to take the air, or to regard the world from the vantage of dusty, unwashed sills! Inevitable, yet with the perversity of cat nature, it was extraordinary how seldom this all-to-be-desired vision burst upon the view. "It's not fair!" Rowena cried. "You have all the poor houses on your side, and poor houses have always more cats than rich ones. A cat for every floor. We ought to change sides between every station, like cricket!"

"Fudge! You've got the open country. Look out for pigs and quarries... We've had no luck with cats for the last three journeys. On the whole, I think yours is the best side."

6

"Why didn't you choose it yourself, then?"

"Charity!" answered Gurth, shortly, with a twinkling glance at his partner, who happened to be at the same time his favourite sister, despite her many and obvious faults. If he had been asked to describe Dreda's character, he would have said in his easy schoolboy language that she was a bit of a sham, perhaps, but then all girls were shams more or less, and if you kept her off high falutin', she was a decent sort, and always ready to do a fellow a good turn.

It was sad to note that even when speaking of his favourite sister, Gurth should have felt it necessary to adopt this tone of patronage, but even the stoutest champion of girls cannot but admit that the sense of honour is in them less developed than in boys, and that in moments of irritation they betray a petty spite, of which the more brutal male is incapable. Gurth was conscious that he had faults of his own, but he regarded them leniently as being on an altogether different level from those of his sisters. He was a bit of a slacker, perhaps, but most "men" were slackers, and yet pulled through all right by means of a spurt at the end. His chiefs called him obstinate, but a fellow had to know his own mind if he were to get on in the world, and he jolly well knew that he was right as often as not Masters were awful muffs. On the other hand, he hated gush like poison, and was invariably a hundred times better than his word, whereas Dreda could hold forth as eloquently as a parson, with the tears pouring down her cheeks, and her figure trembling with emotion, and the next day forget the very cause of her emotion! The girl was like a fire of shavings, quickly lighted, quickly extinguished, and probably the greatest punishment which she could have sustained would have been compelled to carry on one of her many philanthropic schemes to a deliberate conclusion.

They were all stored up in the family archives—the histories of Dreda's charitable enterprises! The factory girl to whom she was going to write regularly every week, and whose address was lost in a fortnight—the collecting cards beyond number, for which, in the first ardour of possession, subscriptions were extorted from every member of the household, and which were rescued from stray hiding-places at the last possible moment and despatched with odd offerings of twopences and threepences from "A Friend" scribbled in, to fill up the empty spaces. Everyone understood that the "friend" was Dreda herself, and that she might be expected to be correspondingly short in tuck money for some time to come! Never a society did Dreda hear of but she panted to become a member on the spot, and never a society but received her resignation, accompanied by a goodly sum in fines, before six months had run their course.

Closeted with parent and teachers, the girl received numberless lectures on the dangers of a thoughtless and unstable character, and was moved to ardent vows of repentance; but, alone with Maud, her confidante and admirer, she was wont to cast a kindly glamour of romance over her own delinquencies. "It's my heart," she would sigh pathetically. "My heart is so sensitive. It's like an Aeolian harp, Maud, upon which every passing breeze plays its melody. I'm a creature of sensibility!" And she rolled her fine eyes to the ceiling, the while Maud snorted, being afflicted with adenoids, and wrinkled her brows in the effort to put her fingers on the weak spot in the argument, the which she felt, but had difficulty in explaining.

"Your heart is hard enough at times!" she said at last. "I suppose the strings get so thin with being everlastingly twanged that they break, and then the breeze can moan as much as it likes without waking a sound. When you let that poor little puppy lie for two days without any food, for instance—"

"You're a beast!" retorted Dreda with fervour. "You don't understand. No one does. I'm misunderstood all round. At any rate I'd rather reach the hilltops sometimes than everlastingly crawl along in the mire, like *some* people I can mention. It's better to have soared and fallen than never to have soared at all!"

Dreda, like most of us, was tender towards her own failings, and resented the criticism of her peers. This afternoon she kept her eyes glued upon the landscape, affecting to be ignorant of Gurth's sly hit, and presently it was balm to her wounded spirit to be able to win the game for herself and her partner, and with a squeal of triumph to point to an upper window in a row of tenement houses, where two erect ears and a pair of yellow eyes could be clearly discerned over the edge of a wooden box filled with miniature fir trees of funereal aspect.

The game was over, and with it had disappeared all disposition to quarrel. Henceforward, to the end of the journey, the four young people chatted amicably together, discussing various subjects of interest, but invariably

8

returning to the one absorbing question of the hour—what could have happened to account for the hasty and mysterious summons to the solitary home in the country at a time when all their interests and pleasures were centred in town?

Chapter Two.

Mr and Mrs Saxon welcomed their children on the threshold of their country home, but a chill seemed to settle on the young people's spirits as they entered the great square hall, which looked so colourless and dreary. As a rule, The Meads was inhabited during the summer months alone, and the children were accustomed to see it alight with sunshine, with doors and windows thrown wide open to show vistas of flower gardens and soft green lawns. In such weather, a house was apt to be regarded merely as a place to sleep in, but now that it would be necessary to spend a great part of the day indoors, it was regarded more critically, and found far from attractive.

The Meads was one of those square, uncompromisingly ugly white houses which are so often to be found in rural England, and which were built at that architecturally unhappy period when old traditions had been cast aside and the modern craze for art was as yet undeveloped. There were plenty of rooms in the house, lofty and spacious enough, but as to outline just so many boxes, with four straight walls, and never a niche or an alcove to break the severity of line. The hall was another square, and the staircase ascended straightly to the first landing, where a monstrosity of a stained-glass window lighted the long corridors beyond.

The furniture was of the same calibre as the house, for, The Meads having been regarded more as a convenient dumping-ground for the children in the summer holidays than as a formal residence, everything that was shabby, injured, or out of date had been weeded from the beautiful town mansion and drafted down to fill up the big square rooms. Mr Saxon had a shooting-box in Scotland in which he was wont to spend the autumn months, Mrs Saxon had a passion for travelling, and could not understand the joy of spending every summer in the same house. The Meads was large, healthy, and convenient, so that while the children were young it had filled a real need, but there was no denying that, regarded as a winter residence, it bore a somewhat chilling aspect. Gurth looked round the hall with eyes very wide open and nose screwed up in eloquent disapproval.

"I say! don't it look different, just, without the sun? Regular old grim hole of a place, ain't it? Like an institution, or a hospital, or something of the kind—not a bit like home—"

"Oh, Gurth, don't," cried his mother quickly, while her forehead corrugated with lines as of actual physical pain. "Dear, you are cold and tired after your journey. Things always look dull when one is tired. Come into the library, all of you! There's a glorious fire, and you shall have tea at once." She slid her hand into her eldest daughter's arm, looking with fond admiration at the fair, delicately cut profile. "You have had a happy time in town this last week—since we left?"

Rowena turned her tall head, and looked down upon her mother with the air of a young goddess, offended, yet resolutely self-restrained. Mrs Saxon was a medium-sized woman, but she looked small beside the tall slenderness of the young daughter who held herself so loftily erect. "Mother!" cried Rowena, in a deep tone of remonstrance, "it's the Vincents' dance to-morrow! I was looking forward to it more than anything else. Lots of grown-up people are going—it would have been almost like coming out. I never thought you would have brought me away from town the very day before *that*. You knew how I should feel—"

"Darling, I'm sorry, more sorry than I can say, but it was necessary. As things are, it is better that you should not go. I'll explain—we will explain. You shall hear all about it later, but first we must have tea. I think we shall all feel better after tea."

Mrs Saxon looked from one to another of her children with the same strained, unnatural smile which had greeted them a few minutes before, and Gurth and Dreda, falling behind the rest, rolled expressive eyes and whispered low forebodings.

"Something up! I thought as much. What can it be?"

"Don't know. Something horrid, evidently. In the holidays, too. What a sell!"

Miss Bruce had considerately disappeared, and the parents and children were left alone in the big bare library, with its rows of fusty, out-of-date books in early Victorian mahogany bookcases, its three long windows draped in crimson red curtains, its Indian carpet worn by the tramp of many feet. A cheerful fire blazed in the grate, however, and the tea equipage set out on the long table was sufficiently tempting to raise the spirits of the travellers. It was a real old-fashioned sit-down tea, where one was not expected to balance a cup and plate on one's knee and yet refrain from spilling tea or scattering crumbs on the carpet. Girls and boys arranged themselves in their usual places with sighs of relief and satisfaction, and, disdaining bread-and-butter, helped themselves energetically to the richest cake on the table. It was a family custom with the Saxons to begin on cake and work steadily back to bread and butter. There had been some opposition to encounter from conservative elders before this reversal of the ordinary programme had been sanctioned, but the arguments advanced had been too strong to resist.

"I can 'preciate things more when I'm hungry. Cake's the best thing; why need I stodge on bread and butter till I can't properly 'preciate the cake? Why can't I stodge on cake, and eat the bread when I don't 'preciate? It doesn't matter about bread!"

So ran the thread of Harold's arguments, and it must be confessed that there was reason therein. To-day, as the young people satisfied their first pangs of hunger on iced cake, the parents watching them exchanged a piteous glance, for the proceeding seemed so sadly typical of the secret that was about to be divulged! Until this day, all that was richest and best in life had been the everyday possession of these loved and fortunate children—after to-day, the love would continue unchanged, but the luxuries must come to an end.

The meal was unusually silent, both Mr and Mrs Saxon and the elder boys and girls being too much oppressed by their own feelings to be able to indulge in ordinary light conversation; only Harold and Maud remained unconscious of the cloud in the atmosphere, and everyone was thankful for their artless prattle, which filled up what would otherwise have been a painful silence. As for the twins, they were quite elated to find so attentive an audience, for as a rule their attempts to enter the conversation were severely nipped in the bud. "That's enough, thank you!" Rowena would say in her most lofty manner. "Shut up, you kids. A fellow can't hear himself speak for your row!" Gurth would call out fiercely. Even when Mrs Saxon was present she would shake her head gently across the table, to enforce the oft-repeated axiom that in so large a family the younger members must perforce learn to be quiet at table. Maud beamed with pleasure at being allowed to continue her never-ending descriptions without a word of remonstrance. She was a fair, pretty, somewhat stupid child, gifted with an overflow of words, which were, however, singularly incapable of conveying any definite impression. Observation she possessed in abundance, but her discursive narratives were by no means improved by being weighted by a plethora of useless detail. One could listen to Maud's efforts to describe her own doings for half an hour on end, and remain almost as much in the dark as at the beginning! On the present occasion she was full of excitement about a wonderful conjurer whose tricks she had witnessed at a children's party in town three nights before, and which she was anxious to enumerate for the benefit of the family.

"...He was the most egg-strawdinary creature you ever saw. He did the most egg-strawdinary things. I'll tell you what he did... You know the Westons' drawing-room? You go upstairs—crimson carpets, and such wide brass rods. Then there's a statue holding up a lamp, and the first door's the drawing-room. All the doors were taken down to make more room, and there were rows and rows of forms... He was like a Frenchman with a pointed moustache, but his clothes weren't very clean... He rolled up his sleeves, and there was a ring on his finger, and yards and yards of ribbon came out of his thumb. He had a little table in front of him with bulgy legs. It stands in the corner with silver on it. Then he asked a boy in the front row for a watch... Mr Weston said he wouldn't have lent *his*, but he got it back all right. It was egg-strawdinary! Meta Rawlins sat by me. She had a pink sash. She says her father can do it a little bit, only of course not as well as this one. Then there was an egg. If he had broken it, it *would* have made a mess on the carpet! Meta said perhaps it was stone. He talked all the time, so funny and quick, and one of his front teeth was out. He asked if any boy or girl would go up to help him, and Brian Hackett went. He looked so silly. He had to hold things in his hand, and when he asked for them, they weren't there. It was egg-strawdinary! We had supper in the dining-room, jellies and cream, and presents in the trifle. I saw the conjurer having his in the library. I never saw anything so egg-strawdinary in all my life!"

Gurth and Hereward exchanged expressive glances, Rowena frowned impatience, Mrs Saxon smiled a faint amusement, and Maud continued to prattle on, blissfully unconscious of the fact that no one troubled to listen.

It was after everyone had been fed and refreshed that the explanation of the mysterious summons from town was given, in response to an outspoken question from Dreda, whose impetuous nature was ever impatient of suspense.

"Mother, what has happened? There must be something, or you would never have left town and sent for us in such a hurry. Can't you tell us now? It's something horrid, of course! And it's horrid waiting for horrid things."

Dreda put both elbows on the table, in flagrant disregard of schoolroom rules, and leant her charming, eager face in the cup of her hands. She might describe her state of mind as "horrid," but an appearance more opposed to such a description it would be impossible to imagine. Dreda had been hungry, and her hunger was satisfied; she had been cold and tired, now she was warmed and refreshed; she talked vaguely of horrible things, but nothing approaching real fear had as yet entered her heart. Grown-ups made such a fuss about trifles. Probably it was something quite silly and unimportant after all.

Mrs Saxon did not answer. She looked down at her hands and twisted the rings on her fingers, the while her husband took upon himself the burden of explanation.

"Yes, Dreda, we wish to speak out plainly. As far as possible we have always taken our children into our confidence, and now we must all try to strengthen each other, for a great change is before us. It must affect us all... I have lost money—a great deal of money. I am no longer a rich man. Your mother and I came down here to face the situation quietly, and to think out our plans. We wished to be by ourselves for a few days before saying anything to you."

"Oh–h. Is that it? Poor father! What a shame!"

"What a beastly fag! How did it happen, Pater?"

"Poor old father! Yes! I *quite* understand."

They spoke together with impetuous warmth, Gurth, Hereward, and Etheldreda, but, in spite of their words, none of them understood in the least. Maud and Harold stared open-mouthed. Only Rowena turned white, and pressed her lips nervously together.

"Thank you, dears. I knew you would sympathise, but our grief is on your account more than on our own. If you can bear the change bravely, our worst fears will be allayed. It will be a big change. To begin with, I have let the town house. An offer came to take it furnished on a lease, and I dared not refuse. The Meads will now be our settled home."

Silence... One definite statement has more effect than a dozen vague forebodings, and the young people sat stunned with dismay, while the thoughts of each wandered away on a voyage of personal reflections.

"No town house! No season! Shut up here all the year round, just as I was coming out, and expecting to have such a lovely time."

"Let the house! Whew! Things must be precious bad ... Suppose, after all, the Governor can't afford to send me to the army!"

"Here's a pretty go! The house doesn't matter. The country knocks town into fits any day, but it will be a beastly fag if we have to cut things down fine. What about the horses?"

"Poor father. Oh, dear, how awful mother looks! Rowena is a brute to look so cross. P'raps the Spider will have to go, and I shall be finished, and done with lessons. Topping!"

"Bateson's father lost his money and he went to sea. I wonder if they'd let me!"

"I've got five pounds six in the bank. I'll draw it out, and give it to them to help. That would last for mumfs and mumfs."

Mrs Saxon lifted her sad eyes and glanced wistfully round the table. When she herself had first heard the news she had been stunned into silence; she hardly expected words, but her mother's heart yearned for a glance of sympathy and love. The boys, as is the habit of boys, were rendered awkward and uncomfortable by the atmosphere of emotion, and stared stolidly at their plates. Rowena sat like a frozen statue of misery, Maud gaped blankly from one face to another; only Dreda was ready and waiting with her sunny smile and her easy flow of sympathy.

"Darling! Of course we'll be brave! Don't worry about us. Everyone says money doesn't matter a bit. You can be perfectly happy without it... Perfectly sickening for you and father, down here by yourselves with all that worry. You must have been bored!"

Bored! The utter inadequacy of the word brought a smile to the parents' eyes, but the kindly warmth of voice and manner was as balm to their sore hearts. What though Dreda's conduct belied her words time and again, her impetuous kindliness of heart was for the moment infinitely soothing, and a blessed contrast to Rowena's gloom. Both parents smiled lovingly upon her, and Dreda glowed with satisfaction. Really, being ruined was quite exciting and dramatic!

"Thank you, Dreda," said her father, gratefully. "These have been very sad days for us, as you say, and even yet we are feeling rather stunned by the suddenness of this trouble, and have not been able to think out definite plans for your future. It was necessary to tell you the bare fact, but you must be patient and forbear from questioning for a few days. We shall not keep you in suspense longer than is necessary."

Suspense! Six pairs of ears pricked uneasily at the sound of that word; six hearers seemed to hear in it the knell of a cherished hope. Even Dreda was awed into silence. The "horrid things" were evidently not yet finished. What was going to happen next?

Chapter Three.

In the schoolroom the young people flocked together, eager to discuss the news apart from the restraint of their parents' presence. Round the great fireplace stood one of those delightful fenders whose top is formed by a wide-cushioned seat. Hereward pulled it forcibly back, with a fine disregard of cinders, until it was sufficiently distant from the blaze to be comfortable, when the six young people seated themselves and prepared to talk in comfort. They made a pretty picture as the leaping flame lighted up their fair blond faces, but for the moment the general expression was far from cheerful. The twins were all eyes and gaping mouths, devoured with curiosity to hear what their elders might have to say with regard to the thrilling intelligence just given; the two schoolboys looked cross and thundery, and it was difficult to say which was the more exasperating to beholders—Rowena's angry frown or Dreda's artificial smiles.

Gurth stamped a smoking cinder into the hearthrug, taking a malicious pleasure in the scorch and smell which ensued. He was never too patient, and this afternoon he felt that he had reached the end of his tether.

"Oh, chuck it, Rowena!" he cried savagely. "What's the use of sitting there looking like a tragedy queen? A jolly example *you* set, for the eldest of a family. You look as if the whole thing was got up on purpose to annoy you, and nobody had a right to be pitied except your precious self. I don't see it a bit! I think you come off best of all. Your education is finished, so you're bound to be all right!"

"Education!" echoed Rowena, in the tone of ineffable scorn natural to a young woman who for months past had been basking in the prospect of a presentation at court. "Education, indeed! Who cares for education? If it *is* finished, what has it all been intended for, pray? To prepare me for a life which I am not to have! Other girls have the best time of their lives when they come out. They are taken about to see everything and do everything which they have longed for all the time they have been shut up at school. It's no wonder I feel bad at coming home to find I have only escaped one prison for another. To live here all the year long! What a prospect! There isn't a decent neighbour nearer than five miles.—If this could only have happened a year or two later, after I had had a *little* fun!"

"Rowena, how selfish! You think only of yourself, and not a bit of anyone else—father or mother, or the boys, or—or Me!" cried Dreda, smiting herself on the breast with dramatic *empressement* as she uttered the last all-important word. "It won't be a bit easier for me when the time comes, but I do *hope* and *believe* that I shall bear it bravely, and try to be an example to the rest. It's our duty, you know, as the eldest daughters of the house!"

"Oh, Dreda, *stop* preaching! It's too ridiculous. *You* to lecture me! For that matter, you need not wait until you are finished to set me an example. You can begin this very minute, for I don't believe for a moment that father will be able to afford to send you to Madame Clerc's. It's a frightfully expensive school, and he used to grumble at the way my extras ran up, even before, when he was rich. I expect you will have to finish at home with the Spider, and then she will go, and you will have to set to work to teach Maud!"

"I shan't!" shrieked Dreda, and flamed a sudden violent red.

"She shan't!" shrieked Maud, at one and the same moment, her fair, placid face flushing to the same crimson hue.

They faced each other like two infuriated turkey cocks—heads erect, feathers ruffled, bodies swaying to and fro with indignation.

"As if I should!"

"As if I'd let you!"

"Teach her!"

"Teach me!"

"The very idea!"

"I'm 'stonished you should talk such nonsense, Rowena!"

Rowena laughed softly. It was the first time she had unbent since the telling of the dread news. She put her head on one side and stared at Dreda's furious face with an "I told you so!" expression which that young lady found infinitely exasperating.

"Our dear Dreda, as usual, finds preaching easier than practice. You see, my dear, when it comes to the point, you are not a bit more resigned than I am myself. It's worse for me to give up all the fun of my first season than for you to stay at home instead of going to school; the only difference is that I have sense enough to realise what is before me, while you are so taken up with sentiment and—"

"Oh, shut up, girls! Stop wrangling, for pity's sake!" cried Hereward, impatiently. "Things are bad enough as they are, without making them worse. If you are going to nag, we'll go downstairs and leave you to yourselves. It's such bad form to kick up a fuss; but girls are all alike. You wouldn't find a boy going on like that—"

Rowena turned upon him with wide, challenging eyes.

"Wouldn't I? Are you so sure? Suppose father were to tell you to-morrow that you couldn't be a soldier, but must go into an office and try to earn money for yourself... Suppose he took you away from Eton, Gurth, and sent you to a cheap school! How would you like that?"

Silence... The two lads sat staring into the fire with dogged faces. They scorned to cry aloud, but the horror of the prospect had for a moment a so paralysing effect that they could not reply. Leave Sandhurst in the middle of one's course, and become—a *clerk*! Leave Eton and the fellows, and go to one of those miserable, second-rate shows which all good Etonians regarded with ineffable contempt! Was it possible to suffer such degradation and live?

Rowena was touched to compunction by the sight of the stricken faces, for though at the moment the worst side of her character was in the ascendant, she was by no means hard-hearted, and, moreover, Hereward was her especial friend and companion. She laughed again, and gave an impatient shrug to her shoulders.

"Oh, don't be afraid ... He never *will*! Whatever happens, nothing will be allowed to interfere with 'the boys' and their careers! We shall all pinch and screw and live on twopence-halfpenny a week, so as to be able to pay your bills. It's always the same story. Everything is sacrificed for the sons."

"Quite right, too," maintained the eldest son, stoutly. "How are you going to keep up the honour of a family if you don't give the boys a chance? It doesn't matter a fig whether a girl is educated or not, so long as she can read and write. She'll marry, of course, and then she has nothing to do but add up the bills."

At this truly masculine distinction, Rowena and Dreda tossed scornful heads and rolled indignant eyes to the ceiling.

"I shall never marry!" announced the former, thinking ruefully of the bare countryside, with never a house of consequence within a radius of miles ... "I am a suffragette. I believe in the high, lofty mission of women!" cried the second, who had been converted to the movement the day before by the sight of some sketches in the *Daily Graphic*. Only nine-year-old Maud sniffed, and opined, "I shall marry a lord! Then he'll have lots of money, and I'll give it to father, and we'll live happily ever after."

Poor Maud! Her millennium was not to begin just yet, at least; for Nannie, her immaculate but austere attendant, rapped at the door at that moment, and summoned her nursling to be bathed and put to bed. Maud was every evening enraged afresh at being called at such a ridiculously early hour, and to-night her annoyance was increased by the fact that she was torn ruthlessly from the rare treat of a conference with her elders, in which she had really been and truly on the level of a "grown-up." She fumed with anger, but presently consolation came with the idea of a dramatic disclosure upstairs. She waited until she and her attendant were alone together in the bedroom, and then sprung the bolt in her most impressive fashion.

"Nannie, we're ruined!"

"Indeed, miss. Sorry to hear it, I'm sure," returned Nannie, unperturbed. It is safe to predict that any important family news will be known as soon in the servants' hall as in the drawing-room, and Nannie had the air of listening to a very stale piece of information.

Maud was distinctly disappointed, but nerved herself for fresh efforts. "Yes. Bankrup'! There's nothing left. I'm going to give up all my savings. What will you do, Nannie—leave?"

"I shall be pleased to stay on, miss, as long as your mother can afford to give me my wages and a nursery maid."

"Oh, Nannie, how *mean*! The Pharisees likewise do as much as that! In storybooks the nurses always stay on, whether they are ruined or not, and give their money to help. You *are* mean!"

"No impertinence, please," said Nannie sharply. She was just beginning to comb out Maud's hair, and it was astonishing how many knots there appeared to be that evening. "I'm sorry I spoke," reflected poor Maud.

Chapter Four.

In the next week future plans were practically settled so far as the young people were concerned. Rowena had been right in her surmise about the boys, for, like most fathers, Mr Saxon was prepared to retrench in any and every direction rather than interfere with the education of his sons. It was a family tradition that the eldest son should go into the army; therefore, at all costs, Hereward must continue that tradition. The Saxons had for generations been Eton boys, therefore it was impossible that Gurth could attend another school. As to the girls—well, Mr Saxon dearly loved his three daughters, and was proud of their grace and beauty, but in effect he held much the same ideas with regard to their education as those which Hereward had expounded to his sisters' indignation. He thought it quite unnecessary to spend large sums on schooling for girls, and for his own part frankly preferred a woman who had no pretensions to being a blue-stocking.

The boys received the intelligence with a complacent sense that all was as it should be, and the one great anxiety being relieved, were disposed to make light of minor privations. What though the manner of living at home must necessarily be less luxurious than of yore, holidays occupied, after all, a small portion of the year, and in a few years' time they would be launching out for themselves. Hereward had an ambition to join an Indian regiment. Gurth was destined for the Civil Service. The Meads would be quite a good old place in which to spend an occasional furlough. But the girls! The girls were by no means reconciled to being sacrificed on the altar of masculine ambition. When the programme for their own future was announced by the nervously anxious mother, Rowena, Etheldreda, and Maud were alike consumed with indignation and dismay. They could hardly believe the evidence of their own ears as they listened to her words:

"Father thought I had better have a little talk with you, dear girls, and explain to you what we have decided about your future. It has been a difficult question—very difficult, and we have had to face alterations which we would thankfully have avoided, for in the end it simply comes down to the bare question of what we can or cannot afford. The boys' education is unfortunately very costly, and those expenses cannot be reduced."

"Why?" demanded Dreda. The crisp, sharp question cut like a lash across Mrs Saxon's soft-toned explanation, and she started, and faced her young daughter with a shrinking almost of dismay. Perhaps in her heart of hearts she, too, doubted the justice of the masculine mandate that girls should invariably be sacrificed for boys, but she was too loyal to admit any dissension when her husband had laid down his commands.

"Why, Dreda?" she repeated, gently. "Because the boys have their way to make in the world ... If we have not much money to leave them, we must at least give them every chance of success. Their education will be their capital."

"An officer in the army needs a large private allowance. Father has always said so. Hereward will need to be helped all his life, instead of being able to help the family as an eldest son should do ... He could go into business."

"Oh, Dreda dear! You, who are so sympathetic and kind-hearted. Think of the terrible disappointment! There always has been a soldier in the family."

"The family has always been rich. Of course I don't want him to be disappointed. I don't want *anyone* to be disappointed," declared Dreda with an emphasis which brought the colour into her mother's thin cheeks. "I suppose I can go to Madame Clerc's at Easter, just the same?"

"I—I am afraid ... Madame Clerc's is a very expensive school, darling. I am afraid it is out of the question! We will do all we can for you. That is one of the principal things which we have had on our minds the last week, and I trust—I believe we have made satisfactory arrangements. Miss Bruce does not feel able to give you finishing lessons, but Mrs Webster, of Swithin, tells me that she is quite satisfied with the school to which she has sent her three daughters. The education is all that could be desired, and the fees much more moderate than Madame Clerc's. We should see more of you, too, darling, for you would be able to come home for the exeats in the middle of the term—"

"Mother! What are you saying? You can't possibly be in earnest. Please, please don't frighten me! It's a hateful school. I have always looked down upon it and detested it, and thanked goodness *I* should never have to go to it!"

Dreda's face was aflame with colour; her eyes had widened until they looked about twice their natural size, in her voice there sounded a quiver of so real a distress that the mother flushed painfully in response.

23

"Dear! why be so prejudiced? It may not be so fashionable a school as Madame Clerc's, but it is admirable in every way, and you will meet friends there whom you already know—the Websters..."

"Know them! We don't! We have met now and then, but we always determine not to know them. We christened them 'The Currant Buns,' and hated them from the first moment. Round, white faces and little curranty eyes!"

"Dreda! Dreda! What has appearance to do with it? You confess yourself that you are prejudiced, so you cannot possibly judge... They are said to be clever and industrious, and exceptionally well brought up, but there will be other girls, plenty of other girls from whom to choose friends."

"It is settled, then? Really *settled*. You have seen the mistress?"

"Yes, dear, it is settled. You are to begin work at the beginning of the term. The Websters are delighted to think of having you as a companion."

Dreda flung out her arms with a gesture of passionate despair, stood for a moment confronting her mother with flashing eyes and quivering lips, then suddenly wheeled round, and rushed headlong from the room.

Her first overwhelming impulse was to get out into the air. The house suffocated her, and besides, she was going to do something ... something desperate ... and there was no scope indoors. She thought of the lake, lying dull and grey within its reedy bank, and saw a vision of herself floating on the surface, with her unbound hair streaming round her face. In the Academy a year before she had been much attracted by a picture of the dead Elaine, and her own hair was exactly the same shade... But it was wicked to commit suicide, and, miserable though she was, life held too many attractions to be lightly abandoned. She would just run away into the darkness and the silence, with her sore, sore heart—to commune with nature, and face the future alone with her own soul! Dreda sobbed aloud at the pathos of the thought, and, racing down the passage, threw open the side door leading into the garden.

A gust of wind blew into her face, a dash of cold sleety rain. The sky was inky black, so black that it was impossible to distinguish even the outline of the trees: the air was soaking with moisture. To one longing for darkness and loneliness, the prospect should have been all that could be desired; yet

Dreda drew back shuddering, and shut the door with a hasty hand. It was wet. She hated to get wet, yet she could not take an umbrella. When your heart was breaking, and you were face to face with one of the tragic moments of life, to walk abroad sheltered by an umbrella was too calm and commonplace a proceeding to be contemplated for a moment! Dreda decided that on the whole it would be better to do her wrestling in her own room; but the noise of the opening and shutting of the door had attracted attention, and as she slowly retraced her steps the pantry door opened, and Martin the parlourmaid thrust her head inquiringly outward.

Martin was a pleasant middle-aged woman, an old retainer in the family, and the pantry at The Meads was quite a good-sized room, and a comfortable one at that, boasting a fireplace in which blazed the cheeriest of fires, for Martin was fond of comfort, and took a pride in keeping her domain spick and span. Her face brightened as she saw the girl standing in the passage, for Dreda was a favourite with all the servants. Miss Rowena, they agreed, was "high;" but Miss Dreda was "feelin'."

"Very feelin' was Miss Dreda!" She was always sorry for you, and wanted to help. They bore her no grudge because the "wanting" frequently went no farther than words. She was but young. Young things did forget. It was entered to her abiding credit that she was "feelin'."

This afternoon one glimpse at the flushed, excited face was sufficient to show that the girl herself was in trouble, and Martin threw open the door to show the hospitable glow of the fire.

"Miss Dreda! Was that you standing by that door in the cold? You'll be catching cold; that's what you'll be doing! I'm having a snack of cocoa and buttered toast. Come in and have a bite by the fire."

Dreda hesitated. Buttered toast was incongruous—painfully incongruous; for among the other desperate resolutions which had rushed through her brain, a slow, determined starvation had held a foremost place. She would turn with a sick distaste from the pleasures of the table; would eat only the plainest of viands, and of them barely enough to keep herself in life. She would grow thin and hollow-eyed, and her parents, looking on, would repent their cruelty in sackcloth and ashes. But—the buttered toast smelt wonderfully good!

"I'll come in and warm myself, but—I'm not hungry," said Dreda, hesitating. But Martin did not appear to have heard. As her young mistress seated herself by the fire, a stool was quietly placed by her side, and on the stool appeared, as if by magic, a plate of toast and a cup of cocoa.

Dreda's hand stretched out involuntarily; she ate and drank, and reflected that, after all, as her father had lost money so unexpectedly, it was only reasonable to suppose that he would recover it in a manner equally rapid. She was sorry she had been cross. She would never be cross any more. In the recovered days of prosperity it would be so pleasant to remember how nobly she had borne herself in the hour of trial!

Chapter Five.

Meantime in the schoolroom upstairs another blow had fallen, and Rowena was quivering beneath the shock of discovering that in Miss Bruce's absence it was she and not Etheldreda who was expected to carry on Maud's education.

"I am sure you will be a conscientious teacher, dear; and I hope that the regular occupation, and the consciousness that you are being of real use will make life brighter for you. Maud will promise to be an industrious pupil, won't you, darling?"

Maud eyed Rowena's tragic countenance, and felt it wise to refrain from rash protestations. She was longing to rush after Dreda to declaim against this last injustice, and as her mother continued to address herself pointedly to Rowena, taking no more notice of her own important presence, she slipped softly from the room.

The two who were left, felt, the one a throb of relief, the other a chill of acute discomfort, at finding themselves alone. The tie between this mother and her eldest daughter was a very tender one, and in the shock of the recent losses Mrs Saxon had unconsciously built much on Rowena's sympathy and love. Rowena would help. Rowena would sympathise; Rowena—herself a woman—would understand some things which even the good husband could not grasp. In the happy, easy days of prosperity, Rowena could always be relied on to be loving, dutiful, and considerate—it was a shock to discover that these good qualities had not enough foundation to withstand the test of adversity. Mrs Saxon was not angry; only distressed and troubled afresh, and overwhelmingly anxious to find the right way to her daughter's heart.

"Mother!" cried Rowena sharply. "*How* did father lose his money? It seems so strange that it should disappear all of a sudden like this. We have always had plenty until now. Has he been speculating, or doing something rash?"

The momentary pause before Mrs Saxon replied and the dignified lifting of her gentle head were more eloquent than a spoken reproof.

"No, Rowena; there is no blame attaching to your father. There has been a great failure in America, which has affected many of his investments. We cannot reproach ourselves for any want of care, and that being so, we must look upon this change of circumstances as coming to us from God's hands, and try to learn the lessons which it is intended to teach. To each of us, perhaps, our own task appears especially hard. You, darling, have looked forward to a time of pleasure and gaiety, and it is difficult to give it up cheerfully, and face living quietly in the country and helping in the house. I understand; I've been a girl myself, and I remember how I felt; but, darling, I am a woman now—getting quite an old woman—and I have learnt my lessons. There is more real joy and contentment to be gained by simply doing one's duty than in all the balls and receptions of a London season, Rowena!"

Rowena sat dumb, her eyes fixed on the tablecloth, her long dark lashes resting on her cheeks. Those were the sentiments you read in books, and heard in sermons, but it was always grown-up people who voiced them; grown-up people who, like mother, had had a good time in their own youth, and were afterwards unreasonable enough to expect their children to be resigned and middle-aged when they had just emerged from the schoolroom. Rowena thought of the prospect which had stretched dazzlingly before her but a week before; of the gaiety and variety of amusement which had made so fair a dream, and contrasted it with the prospect of an uneventful domestic life at the Manor—teaching Maud! She pressed her lips together, and sat silent, feeling her mother's eyes on her face; dreading to meet their tenderly reproaching gaze.

"That sounds strange to you, dear, and perhaps a little hard, but all the same it is *true*. I do not minimise your disappointment, but for the time being it is inevitable, and nothing remains but to face the situation bravely. As the eldest daughter of the house more depends upon you than upon any of the rest, and your opportunities will be endless. You can be a great comfort to us, darling, or a great additional care. It all depends upon the spirit in which you start the new life—upon whether you look in or out— put yourself first, or think of others."

Mrs Saxon paused again, and within Rowena's still form two contending forces fought for victory. While one sullen spirit held her dumb, the real self seemed to stand apart, reviewing her own conduct, and uttering words of exhortation and appeal: "How hateful of you never to say a word in reply! Poor mother! her voice trembled... It's hard on her, too. If you could just put your arms round her neck and kiss her, and promise to be good, it would comfort her ever so much. And you'd be happier yourself. It only makes you more miserable to sulk, and be unkind. Look up and smile, and promise to be nice." So urged the inner voice, but alas, the fleshy eyelids seemed heavy as lead, and the lips remained stiff and unmoveable. To all outward appearance there was no sign of softening in the fixed face.

Mrs Saxon's heart sank heavily. Rowena's lack of response to her appeal was a bitter disappointment; but she realised that it was useless to prolong the interview. A few moments longer she waited, hoping against hope for a word in reply, then stifling a sigh, she rose from her seat.

"Well—I must go back to father. Look after the fire, darling, if you are going to stay here. It is getting low, and you must not catch cold."

She bent as she passed to kiss the unresponsive lips, and walked from the room carrying a heavy heart in her breast. "If she had only spoken! If she had even looked up and smiled!" Such was the wounded mother cry; and all the time Rowena's heart was speeding unspoken messages after her as she went.

"Mother! I'm sorry. You are so sweet, and I am a wretch! I *will* try! I'll try my best!"

Alas! the ears of sense could not catch the message, and so the opportunity passed, and left both hearts aching and oppressed.

Chapter Six.

"What's 'rejuiced'?" queried Maud, squeezing herself into the central place on the big fender, as her brothers and sisters sat roasting chestnuts by the schoolroom fire one wet afternoon a few days later, and the question being received by a blank stare of bewilderment she repeated the word with intensified emphasis. "*Re-juiced! We're* rejuiced! I heard Mary say so in the schoolroom. She said to nurse that she didn't know if the missis would be wanting to keep on two housemaids now she was re-juiced! Does it mean *poor*?"

"You have no business to listen to servants' conversation; but if you do, pray spare us the repetition!" said Rowena in her most grown-up manner. Maud reflected that ever since mother had spoken of the new arrangement about lessons, Ro had talked exactly like a governess, and been just as snappy as snappy. She bounced on her seat, and wagged her head in the obstinate manner which she adopted upon provocation.

"I don't listen, but I have ears, and if people speak I am obliged to hear. Mary came into the room to dust. Nurse was darning the tablecloth. It's all gone into holes where Gurth spilt the chemical acid. It's the one with the little shamrocks for a pattern. So Nurse said: 'Drat those boys!' and licked the cotton with her tongue, and—"

Hereward and Gurth exchanged glances of resigned boredom, but Dreda drummed her heels on the floor, and called aloud with startling emphasis:

"Go on! Go on! Who wants to hear about tablecloth patterns, and licking threads? Keep to your point, if you have a point to stick to! If Rowena's is going to give you lessons, she'd better begin by teaching you not to be such a bore. You go prosing on and on—"

"I don't. I'm not. Bore yourself! 'Twas most intrusting!" insisted Maud, stolidly. "They were sort of talking about us all, in a sort of way as if I couldn't understand, and I understood all the time, and they said we were rejuiced, and I asked you a simple question what it meant. When you're perlite to other people, other people should be perlite to you in return."

"All right, Maud, keep calm, keep calm! You reduce a thing by taking something from it. We are reduced because something—a great deal—has been taken away from our income, and what remains is not enough to go

30

round. I expect the second housemaid will be sent packing, and you will have to make the beds."

Maud squealed with dismay, then with a gleam of shrewdness nodded her head, and prophesied sagely:

"It would be worse for you than me if I did! I'd make them full of crumples. I'd get hold of the ends of the clothes, and *Hop* them down all together like Mary does when it's her Sunday out, and she's in a hurry. *Then* you'd be in a rage when you got in and your toes stuck out!"

"I'll make the beds!" announced Dreda, graciously. "I think all girls ought to learn to be domestic, and there's a real art in making beds. I've often thought how much better I could do it than any servant we have had. It's the trained intellect, I suppose. (I do *hate* you, Rowena, when you sneer like that!) F'rinstance—I like my blankets just up to my chin, and if I tell Mary ten times a day, it's always the same—she doubles them down till you are all hunkley round the neck. Then that leaves less to tuck in at the bottom, and if you have a nightmare and kick, there you are with your feet sticking out in the cold, and have to get up and tuck them in, when you want to sleep! And I can't endure creases. I like the under sheet stretched as tight as tight. Everyone likes a bed made in a special way, and it *ought* to be done. Think of the time one spends in bed! A third of one's life. It's a shame not to be comfortable. I should be an expert in bed-making. I'd keep a book to remind me of everyone's special fancies—"

"And lose it the second day! Play all the experiments you like, but leave my room alone. I want no expert. The ordinary common or garden housemaid is good enough for me," said Hereward, cruelly.

Dreda reflected sadly that a prophet was not a prophet in her own country, but she was too much fired with the new idea to relinquish it without a trial. Besides, hidden in her heart lay the reviving thought: "If I could prove that I could be of use in the house, perhaps they'd let me stay! I know quite enough lessons as it is!"

The first two nights after hearing of the changed arrangements for her own education Dreda had cried herself to sleep, and had even succeeded—with a little difficulty—in squeezing out a few tears as she dressed in the morning, or what was the use of breaking your heart if no one were the wiser, or pitied you for your pathetic looks? By the third morning, however, her facile nature had adapted itself to the inevitable. She was tired of being in the dumps, and reflected that with a little diplomacy she would be able to "manage" the school governesses as cleverly as she had done the Spider before them, while the Currant Buns looked meek, poor-spirited creatures, who would like nothing better than to be ruled. "*I'll* teach them!" prophesied Dreda darkly, and the word was used in no educational sense.

The future was thus swallowed at a gulp; but all the same Dreda thought it worth while to interview her mother on the subject of her domestic ambitions, and was much disappointed to have her generous offer kindly but firmly refused.

"There is no necessity, dear. Thank you very much, all the same," Mrs Saxon said, smilingly. "We are no longer able to keep up two houses, but we can afford all the help that is needed for one. The two housemaids can keep the bedrooms in order very easily in this fresh clean air."

Etheldreda put her head on one side and lengthened her upper lip, after a fashion she affected when she wished to be impressive.

"*Still*," she insisted, obstinately, "when a family is reduced in circumstances I think it *most* important that the girls should learn to be domestic. I have always understood that in reduced circumstances it was necessary for the mistress to overlook *everything*, and how can you learn to do that if you never begin? It seems to me that one can never begin too young, and if we *could* do with only one housemaid, it is our duty to do so."

Mrs Saxon laughed. She always did laugh when Dreda waxed impressive, which was one of that young woman's trials in life.

"Darling Dreda!" she cried, affectionately. "You shall be as domestic as ever you please—the more domestic the better; but there is a time for everything, and this is your time for study. You must wait until your education is finished, before you take up home duties. We are not going to sacrifice your interests for the sake of a servant's wages. Work hard, and do your best, dear. One thing at a time, and that done well—"

But Dreda refused to be convinced.

"*My* theory," she announced, firmly, "my theory is that it is stupid to waste time learning things which you will never need! As we are 'rejuiced' (the expression had stuck, until the very pronunciation was unconsciously reproduced), and I can't go to Madame Clerc's and be finished properly, I should consider that it would be wiser to stop as I am. I am very well grounded. We can't afford to go into society now, so I shall probably marry a man in a humble position, and it's foolish to educate me above my rank!"

"Oh, Dreda, Dreda! Oh! I haven't laughed for weeks. You mustn't be vexed with me for laughing, dear—it's *so* refreshing!" And Mrs Saxon wiped her eyes and chuckled irresistibly, the while her young daughter regarded her more in pity than in anger.

"I can't see what I have said that is so amusing. I was speaking *most* seriously. I'm fifteen. It's my own future that is at stake. Really, mother!"

"I'm sorry, dear, and I don't mean to be unsympathetic. I know you are in earnest, but for the next few years you must consent to be guided by what father and I believe to be best. Whatever may be before you, it is necessary that you have a good education, so put your heart into your work, and get on as quickly as possible."

Dreda sucked her upper lip in eloquent disgust.

"Parents are so *trying*!" she told herself, mentally. "They never seem to think it possible that you know better yourself. I shall be quite different with my daughters. What a pity it is that you can never manage to be your own mother!"

Chapter Seven.

During the next three weeks the Saxons settled slowly into the routine of life as it would in future be spent at the Manor. To begin with, the house itself was greatly improved in appearance by the addition of extra furniture and draperies sent down from the lavishly equipped house in town. The cold austerity of the entrance-hall was turned into something positively approaching cheerfulness by the presence of crimson portières, a huge tapestry screen shutting off the staircase, and, best of all, by a brass brazier which, piled high with blazing coals, diffused both light and heat, and seemed to speak a cheery welcome to each new-comer. The Bechstein grand piano was not only a gain from a musical point of view, but made a decided improvement in the sparsely furnished drawing-room, while a few good pictures and ornaments gave a homelike air which had hitherto been conspicuous by its absence.

Rowena regarded these improvements with the numb unconcern which a prisoner might manifest over an unimportant alteration in his cell; but Dreda, as usual, was afire with enthusiasm, and spent a radiantly happy day playing the part of a charwoman, in apron and rolled-up sleeves. She washed all the ornaments, exulting in the inky colour of the water after the operation, and insisting that each member of the household should ascend to regain the same.

"Isn't it beautifully dirty?" she cried in triumph. "I scrubbed them with the nail brush. You should have seen the dust come out of the chinks! I simply dote upon seeing the water turn black. It's no fun washing things unless they are *really* dirty!"

When the additions were viewed as a whole, however, Dreda was not so content. She even frowned with displeasure at sight of the luxury in the hall.

"It's not consistent!" she pronounced, judicially. "We are *rejuiced*, and it doesn't look rejuiced! People in the neighbourhood coming to call will think we are richer instead of poorer. You will have to explain, mother. It wouldn't be honest if you didn't."

Mrs Saxon's smile was a somewhat painful effort.

"I imagine there will be little need of explanation, Dreda. News flies fast in a country place, and our neighbours probably know our affairs as well as we know them ourselves."

"And are gossiping about us behind our backs, and longing to call and see how we bear it!" continued Rowena, with that new edge of bitterness in her voice, which sounded so sadly in her mother's ears. It needed a hard struggle with herself before Mrs Saxon could command herself to reply gently:

"Curiosity is natural, perhaps, but I don't think we need fear anything unfriendly. If there should be any exhibition of the sort, it's a comfort to feel that I can depend upon my grown-up daughter to set an example of dignity and self-restraint. My nature is like Dreda's, so much more impulsive, that you will be a great strength to me, dear."

Oh, that soft answer that turneth away wrath, how omnipotent it is! The sneer was wiped off Rowena's face as by a sponge, her blue eyes glistened, and she stooped her tall young head to press an impetuous kiss upon her mother's cheek. For the rest of the day she was her old, sweet loving self, and the mother was rewarded a thousandfold for the effort which it had cost her to repress a hasty retort, and replace it by a word of tenderness and appreciation.

At the end of a fortnight the three boys returned to school, placidly resigned to a change of circumstances which left their own lives untouched; and no sooner had they departed than the Spider in her turn began to pack her boxes, in preparation for her own exit. For the past ten years she had been regarded as a member of the family, spending the greater number of her holidays with her pupils, and being included in all the household festivities and rejoicings. It was inevitable that her absence would cause a blank, and the young people experienced sundry pangs of conscience as they recalled the want of appreciation with which they had received their efforts on their behalf. How they had teased and lazed, and plotted and schemed, to escape the tasks which she had so laboriously enforced! How they had laughed behind her back, imitating her little mannerisms, and exhorting each other after her invariable formulae: "Impertinence, my love, is *not* wit!"

"A young lady should be composed and dignified in demeanour."

"Concentration, my dear, concentration! That is what you require." Poor, dear, good Spider; her methods were somewhat behind the times; but she was the kindest, most faithful of souls. Everyone was thankful to know that owing to the recent receipt of a legacy she was able to retire comfortably from active work, and to look forward to a peaceful contented home in the family of a beloved niece. Neither was it a very serious parting, since nothing was so certain as that so true a friend must return again and again to the scene of her labours; to see Hereward in his first uniform; to attend Rowena's marriage; Dreda's coming out; and inspect the progress of her youngest pupils. A few tears were shed when the hour of parting actually arrived, but there was no bitterness in them on either side, nor were they of any long duration.

And now for Etheldreda's turn! When the morning dawned on which she was to depart for school, she felt it fitting that her toilette should express the melancholy of her mood. Dreda had a great idea of fitness, and a costume composed of an old shepherd plaid skirt, a grey flannel blouse and a black tie seemed admirably symbolic of what she herself described as "the mourning of her soul." When it was donned, however, the result was found to be so extremely unbecoming that resolution wavered, and collapsed. After all, the most important matter was to impress her new companions, and there was no denying that that could be done most effectively in blue—in just such a blue as was at that moment hanging in the wardrobe ready for use. With light-like speed Dreda shed her dun-coloured garments on to the floor, and in a trice was arrayed in her prettiest, most becoming costume.

This time the reflection was so pleasing that it was quite an effort to pull down her chin, and drop her eyelids, with the air of melancholy resignation which she was determined at all costs to preserve during breakfast. Mrs Saxon's face brightened at sight of the pretty blue dress, but neither she nor any other member of the family mentioned the fatal word "school." Rather did each one try to give a cheerful turn to the conversation, and to lead it towards a discussion of those topics in which the heroine of the day was the most interested. "Sops!" murmured Dreda dramatically to herself. "Sops!" She struggled hard to restrain her longing for a second helping of bacon; but her courage gave out at the thought of the motor drive across the cold open country.

"I must strengthen myself with plenty of nourishment," she decided, as she handed over her plate, and accepted the offer of a third cup of coffee. Like all pleasant things, however, the meal came to an end at last, and then the great event of the day could no longer be ignored. Maud caught the glance exchanged between her parents, and felt herself freed from her promise of silence.

"*Now!*" she exclaimed, with a gusty sigh of relief. "Now for the Buns! *Now* you'll see which knows most, them or you. Them, I should think, 'cause they're clever, and you forget. Miss Bruce said your head was like a sieve. Do you remember the day she said it? She had on her jet chain, and jingled with the beads. You'll have to remember not to forget, or you'll be the bottom of the class. Fancy three Currant Buns on top!"

She stopped short, with her characteristic throaty little laugh, and Dreda glared at her with flashing eyes. It was really extraordinary that anyone so stupid as Maud should so often succeed in hitting upon just the most aggravating thing to say under the circumstances. Three Currant Buns on top indeed! Life would only be endurable if she herself could seize the leading place, and hold it relentlessly to the end. She would not condescend to reply, and Maud was hurriedly nudged, and poked, and "shoved" into silence by Rowena, who was in an unusually sympathetic mood, realising how she herself would have felt had fate cast her own scholastic lot with that of the Misses Webster.

"Never mind her," she whispered, consolingly, as she followed Dreda upstairs to put on hat and jacket before her departure. "It's not worth while troubling yourself about Maud's remarks. It's impossible to think that any of those girls will get the better of *you*! It's hateful, of course; but perhaps it may not be quite so hateful as we think—"

"Oh, I don't mind. I'm resigned! One can only be as miserable as one can. Perhaps I'll have an accident some day, riding over those rough roads, and then it will all be finished. I don't mind how soon my life is over!" declared Dreda, harpooning her hat viciously with a pin of murderous length, ornamented at the head by a life-size imitation of a tomato. "But while I *do* live, I tell you one thing, Rowena, I'll—I'll *hold my own!*"

"I'm sure of that," assented Rowena, with conviction. "Look here, Dreda, would you like me to drive over with you as well as mother? I could, you know; and it might break the ice!"

"No, no! Father wanted to come, but I begged not. Everything is arranged, and I don't want people looking on. It will be a *hidjus* ordeal!"

"Oh, my dear, come! Don't exaggerate. It's not so tragic as all that."

"Isn't it, then? Don't be so grown-up and horrid! How would *you* like it yourself, if anyone made the best of your having to teach Maud?"

That one trenchant question was sufficient to reduce Rowena to the depths of silent despair, and the two sisters descended the staircase with aspects equally lugubrious and mournful.

It was not a cheerful send-off, despite all the efforts of the family, who stood shivering in the porch to wave farewells, and call out encouraging prognostications so long as the motor remained in sight. Dreda drew a big sigh of relief as they turned out of the drive, and spun rapidly along the highway. The necessity for keeping up a part was over, and involuntarily she began softly whistling beneath her breath, for in truth she was by no means so miserable as she had striven to appear.

Novelty was the breath of Dreda's nostrils. Any novelty to her was better than none, and if the chance of returning to the house had at that moment been vouchsafed, it is doubtful if she would have accepted it at the cost of missing the excitements of the next few hours.

The car spun along strongly, so that the twenty miles' distance was speedily covered, and before Etheldreda was half-way through her dreams it had turned in at a gate, and there before her eyes lay Grey House, a square, pretentious-looking building, with a door in the middle and a stretch of three windows on either side. There, also—oh! thrilling and exciting moment—pressed against the panes of an upper window were a number of round white discs, which must obviously be the faces of pupils watching the advent of the new girl!

Dreda sat up, and throwing back her golden mane, tossed a laughing remark to her mother—the first she had volunteered since leaving home, and showed her white teeth in a determined smile. If she were fated to arrive at all, she would arrive as a conqueror who would be regarded with envy and admiration. Privately, she might consider herself a martyr, but that was not a rôle in which she chose to appear before other people. She was smiling as she entered the drawing-room after her mother, smiling as Miss Bretherton came forward to greet them, smiling still, a forced, fixed smile, as she listened to the conversation between the two ladies.

"Hope we shall be very happy together—"

("I shan't. I don't like you a bit! Scraggy, cross-looking thing! Your nose looks as if it would cut!")

"...Dreda is fond of society. She will enjoy working with other girls!"

("Shan't, then! I shall hate it. I should have enjoyed it in Paris.")

"...Beginnings always are a little difficult; but young people *soon* adapt themselves!"

("It's easy to talk!")

After a few minutes passed in the exchange of these and similar commonplaces, Mrs Saxon rose to depart. On a previous visit she had been shown over the house, and had seen the room where her daughter was to sleep, and now her presence would only prolong the agony. She cast a look at her daughter, full of yearning mother love and sympathy; but Dreda was smiling still, her grey eyes wide open, her very gums showing in the unnatural stretching of her lips. She submitted to be kissed, but offered no caress in return, and turned with a nonchalant air to examine the photographs on the mantelshelf, while Miss Bretherton escorted her mother to the door.

They were all photographs of girls—old girls who had left school and could afford to be amiable and forgiving. One wore a cap and gown and was evidently a crack pupil who had won honours at college; another held a baby on her knee—she was pretty, and had married young; a third supported her head on her hand and stared dreamily into space; another posed against a screen. Dreda stared at them with eyes that grew misty and unseeing, as the motor puffed down the drive. Now she was alone— away from home for the first time in her life! Miss Bretherton was coming back—Miss Bretherton with the thin face and the sharply pointed nose.

The door opened; the photographs looked mistier than ever; Miss Bretherton's voice sounded from an immense distance, saying in cheery tones:

"Now I am going to take you upstairs to see your room, Etheldreda. Susan Webster and Nancy West will share it with you. Susan you know already—a delightful girl; and Nancy is equally charming. Most of the girls returned last night, but we have not yet settled into regular work: it takes a little time to arrange the classes. Are your boots quite clean? Better rub them once more on the mat! Pupils are not allowed to ascend the staircase in outdoor shoes."

She led the way forward, while Dreda followed, looking about with curious eyes. The carpet lasted only so long as the stair could be seen from the hall beneath, and was then replaced by oil-cloth, worn to a colourless drab by the tramp of many feet. On the first storey a narrow passage ran the whole length of the house, and innumerable doors seemed to open on each side. The murmur of voices could be heard from within, as one passed these closed portals; but one of the number, labelled Number 5, was not quite shut, and Dreda had a shrewd suspicion that it opened an inch or two wide as she passed by. Probably it gave entrance to the room from which faces had stared out on the drive; probably the same curious faces were peering forth through that crack at this very moment.

The bedroom bore a bleak look, despite the fact that the furniture was all in threes—three narrow beds, three washstands, three chests of drawers—topped by miniature mirrors—and three small cane-seated chairs. Each of the three inmates had a portion of the room to herself, and against the wall stood two folding screens, evidently designed to insure privacy. Dreda noted with dismay that the two ends of the room, the one next the window and the one next the door, already bore signs of occupation. Her brow clouded, and instead of the usual polite remarks of approval, out shot an impetuous question:

"Have I to take the middle? I'd rather have an end!"

"Susan and Nancy have occupied the same beds for the last year. All are equally comfortable."

"There ought to be three screens. I want two to shut myself in. Suppose one of the others didn't want hers up!"

"Why suppose disagreeables, my dear? It is a great mistake. I feel sure your companions will consider your comfort as thoughtfully as their own. Hang your jacket on the pegs; then you can come to your classroom, to be introduced to your companions. Take off your hat."

Dreda pulled a face in the mirror. She felt cross and ill-used. At home she was accustomed to a big, beautiful room all to herself; she did not at all enjoy the prospect of owning a third of this chill grey dormitory. She took off her hat—conscious that Miss Bretherton's eyes were regarding the tomato-topped pin with silent disapproval—wriggled out of her coat, and bestowed a series of pats and pulls to hair, necktie, and blouse. Being one of the happy people who feel cheered rather than depressed by the sight of her own reflection in the glass, she followed the head mistress downstairs without any of the trepidations of nervousness which afflict most new girls, and was by no means surprised when that lady made straight for the doorway of Number 5.

It opened, and six girls were discovered seated before a table, wearing expressions of preternatural solemnity. One of the number wore spectacles; a second had a broad band of metal over her front teeth; a third had red hair and a thick powdering of freckles; "The Currant Buns" wore dresses of yellowy-brown tweed, which in Dreda's eyes made them appear "bunnier" than ever. So much was taken in by the first lightning glance, as at the appearance of Miss Bretherton the girls leapt mechanically to their feet and stood stolidly at attention.

"Girls, this is your new companion, Etheldreda Saxon. She is to share Number 20 with Susan and Nancy, and I expect will be in the fourth form. You had better leave your books and have a little chat beside the fire, until Miss Drake is ready. You may tell her that I gave you permission."

She left the room and shut the door behind her, and Dreda was left face to face with her new companions.

Chapter Eight.

For a moment the six girls retained their former positions, staring with blank, expressionless faces at the new comer. Then Mary Webster, the eldest of the "Currant Buns," advanced with outstretched hand, followed by her two younger sisters.

"How do you do?"

"How do you do?"

"How do you do?"

"So glad to see you."

"So glad—"

"Very glad—"

The murmurs died into silence, while Dreda smiled a radiant encouragement.

"Quite well, thank you. But rather cold. May we poke the fire? My feet—"

She tapped expressively on the floor, whereupon Mary Webster poked discreetly at the fire and Susan, the youngest of the sisters, pushed a chair into the cosiest corner. The other three girls had come forward by this time, and introduced themselves in due form.

"How do you do? I'm Barbara Moore. It's hateful to be a new girl!"

"How do you do? I'm Norah Grey. Sorry you're cold."

"How do you do? I'm Nancy. Tell me truthfully—*Do you snore?*"

Dreda laughed gaily.

"Sometimes—when I lie on my back. I do it on purpose, because you dream such thrilling dreams. And I yell horribly when I come to the bad bits."

"Something will have to be done!" said Nancy, darkly. She was the girl with the band over her front teeth. It was ugly, but fascinating; one felt constrained to look at it, and looking at it could not help noticing how curved and red were the lips, how darkly lashed the long grey eyes. Nancy was evidently a person to be reckoned with. She sat herself down by the fire, stretched out her feet to the blaze, and appeared to be lost in thought. Dreda longed to talk to her, to inquire what she meant by that mysterious "something," but the "Currant Buns" were clustering round her, regarding her with anxiously proprietary airs as if, having the honour of a personal acquaintance, it was their due to receive the first attention. Dreda felt quite like a celebrity, on the point of being interviewed by a trio of reporters; but as usual she preferred to play the part of questioner herself.

"Were you doing prep when I came in? What classes are you taking to-day? I feel as if I've forgotten everything. One always does in the holidays, doesn't one? Such a bore having to grind through it all again. Seems such a waste of time."

"Have you a bad memory? Miss Drake, our English governess, is especially clever at developing the powers of memory. And holiday tasks are so useful, too; don't you find them so? It is impossible to forget, if one has to study for an elaborate thesis."

"The—what?" questioned Dreda blankly. "But whoever *does* study in the holidays? I don't! If you did, they wouldn't be holidays. So stupid! Holidays are for rest and fun. Bad enough to have lessons for two-thirds of the year. One's brain must have *some* rest!"

She ended on quite an indignant note, and her companions stared at her with a mingling of admiration and dismay. Such a vivid bit of colouring had not been seen for many a long day in that neutral-tinted room. Yellow hair, pink cheeks, red lips, blue dress—she was positively dazzling to behold. The two younger Miss Websters appeared absorbed in admiration, but the eldest and cleverest-looking of the three pursed up her lips with an air of disapproval and said primly:

"It depends upon one's *idea* of rest, doesn't it? Leisure may mean only a time of amusement, but it's a rather poor conception of the word. The ancient Greeks understood by it a time of *congenial* work, as distinguished from work which they were obliged to do. Their necessary work was undertaken in order that they might obtain a time of leisure, but when it came, instead of wasting it in foolish and passing amusement, they used it to strengthen their intellect and to store up ennobling thoughts."

"How did they do that, pray?" Dreda put the question with the air of one launching a poser, but Mary Webster showed no signs of discomfiture.

"They used to meet together in little companies, and discuss the deepest and most important topics of the day—"

"I expect they gossiped horribly!"

"And they watched the dramas—"

"I call that amusement! I wouldn't mind doing that myself."

"But the Greek dramas were not light and vapid like modern plays. They dealt with serious subjects, and the audience often used to commit the words to memory as a mental exercise."

Dreda yawned.

"Ah, well," she conceded indulgently, "it's a long while ago! One mustn't be hard on them, poor dears, for they knew no better. I don't approve of girls bothering their heads about ancient Greeks. Boys have to, for examinations, but if we want to grow up nice, domesticated women it's better to learn modern things, and leave those old fusties alone. They do one no good."

The girls stared at her in stunned surprise. Agnes, the second Webster, dropped her chin to an abnormal length; the youngest, Susan, bit nervously at her lips; Mary cleared her throat and showed signs of returning to the attack, but Dreda was already tired of the subject, and made a diversion by leaping from her seat and approaching the table where piles of blue-covered exercise books were neatly arranged at intervals of about a yard apart.

"Let me look at your books, and see what you are doing! I didn't bring any books till I saw what you used. I expect they will be the same. All school books are. I've got the ones Rowena used." She broke off, staring with dismay at the underlined questions which met her eye in one of Agnes's neatly written books:

"Characterise the work of Praxiteles, comparing it with that of Phidias."

"Describe the Caryatids of the Erectheum."

"*More* Greeks! How awful! You seem saturated in Greece." She threw down the book impatiently and took up another. "Write a short essay on Chaucer (I know Chaucer!) and his times (When did he live? Ages ago, I know, for he couldn't spell), dwelling on (1) the state of society as shown by the attitude of Wycliffe to the Pope, and the higher clergy; (2) the peasants' revolt"— Dreda looked round with horrified eyes. "*What*a thing! Do you often have essays like that? Your governess must be a man in disguise!"

"She is exceedingly clever and well read, and a most interesting and original teacher."

"Humph!—I prefer the old school! Our governess gives us essays on Spring, and Happiness, and quotations from poetry. They are far better, for if you don't know anything, you can make it up. You know the sort of thing. 'One has often felt—' 'Should we not all—' 'At this season of the year our hearts overflow—' I assure you I have often sat down not knowing what on earth I was going to say, and have written *pages*! That's far better for you than learning dull facts about people who were dead and buried hundreds of years ago, because it exercises your imagination and resource, and they are so useful for a woman. Now, just suppose you were married, and a lot of dull people were coming to dinner—it would help you awfully if you'd been trained to make conversation out of nothing! And supposing you suddenly found that there was nothing to eat, and you had to make a dinner out of scraps—what would be most useful to you then, Greek history or a good, resourceful brain?"

Mary and Agnes stared aghast, but the sound of a snigger came from the fireplace where Susan stood meekly in the background, and a moment later a ringing laugh drew all eyes to the doorway where stood a tall, bright-haired girl, whose white teeth gleamed pleasantly through her parted lips.

"Bravo!" she cried gaily. "Bravo, my new pupil! Very adroitly argued. But suppose now that one of your dull diners happened to be an enthusiast about Greece, and that its glories were the only subject on which he was prepared to talk! Suppose he spoke of the 'Caryatids,' for example, and you had no idea what the word meant—how would you keep up your share of the conversation?"

"Quite easily. I'd say—'Really! How very interesting! *Pray* do go on!' Then he'd be charmed. People always are charmed to go on talking," declared Dreda smiling back with the utmost frankness into the face of this bright, friendly stranger.

So this was the English governess of whose cleverness and accomplishments she had heard so much! She looked quite young—ridiculously young; not many years older than Rowena herself. Dreda had expected to see an elderly, spectacled dame, thin and spare, with scant locks dragged tightly back from her face. In the dark depression of her spirits she had thought it possible that she might even wear knitted mittens, and have cotton wool in her ears. Never for a moment had it occurred to her that an accomplished finishing governess could be young and pretty!

To judge from Miss Drake's expression she was experiencing very much the same pleasure in the sight of her new pupil, for her eyes brightened visibly as she looked Dreda up and down, down and up, with a keen, intent scrutiny. She laughed as she heard the girl's answer, and replied easily:

"That's quite true, Etheldreda. I am myself! That's one of the reasons which induced me to work—for unless one is contented to play the part of hearer through life, it really is worth the trouble to store up a little general knowledge, so that one may talk as interestingly as possible. Lessons may seem dull and unnecessary at the time, but they *are* useful afterwards! Now, girls, take your places! Etheldreda shall sit here on my left, and I will read over the syllabus for this term's study, and draw out a timetable. As we come to each fresh subject I will show you our books, Etheldreda, and we will see if they are the same as those which you have been using, and how far you have progressed. I expect we shall be able to work along together, even if there is a little space to be gulfed on either side."

"Please!" cried the new pupil earnestly, "don't call me Etheldreda. Nobody ever does except when I'm in disgrace, and it's so long and proper. I'm always Dreda at home."

"Dreda, then! It *is* more get-at-able. Well, now, Dreda, take a pen and write down our syllabus in this book. I like my pupils to have a clear idea of the work ahead."

Dreda settled herself complacently to the task, but as she wrote her face grew ever longer and longer. What subjects were there which she was supposed to study? Political economy—she had not the vaguest idea of what it meant! Physiology—that was something horrid about one's body, which ought properly to be left to nurses and doctors! Zoology—animals! She knew everything that she wanted to know about animals already; how to feed and tend them, and make them tame and friendly. She could not love them half so much if she were obliged to worry herself learning stupid names half a yard long, which no ordinary human creature understood! Latin—Algebra—Astronomy. She glanced round the table and beheld Mary and Agnes and Susan scribbling away with unruffled composure. No sign of alarm could be traced on their calm, bun-like countenances, the longest words flowed from their pens as if such a thing as difficulty in spelling did not exist. Dreda looked for a moment over Mary's shoulder, and beheld her writing a diphthong without so much as turning a hair.

A chilly feeling crept up her spine; her heart seemed to stop beating, then at the next moment thudded violently against her side. She was not going to be at the top of the class; she was to be at the bottom! Instead of leading the van, and victoriously trailing the Currant Buns in her wake, the Currant Buns would have to trail her; and a heavy, unenlightened load she would be! A stormy prospect lay ahead; straits of difficulty; seas of depression; oceans of humiliation. Pride, and pride alone, prevented Dreda from laying down her head on the dingy brown tablecloth and bursting into tears. Alas, alas! for the happy, easy days of History, Geography, and Arithmetic, with the old-fashioned Spider. Alas for the finishing joys of Madame Clerc's select academy, where the young ladies were taken about to see the sights of Paris, with no other restriction on their pleasure seeking but that on one and all occasions they should amuse themselves in French!

It grew wearisome to make ever the same reply to Miss Drake's question. "No, she had never studied that subject."

"No, she had never seen this book." Mary stared unblushingly with her little dark eyes. Agnes dropped her chin until it looked twice its natural length, Susan flicked over the pages of her exercises and appeared absorbed in their contents. Nancy smiled a furtive smile.

"No," cried Dreda desperately. "No, I know nothing about it! I—I have been educated on quite different lines—I think I had better go on as I have begun. I don't want to keep back the whole class. Let the others go on as usual, and leave me out. I can join *in* for the ordinary subjects."

"Nonsense, Dreda. Nothing of the sort. We take up each subject afresh at the beginning of the term, and if you work hard you will be able to manage quite well. It is better to make a little push to keep in this form than to go into a lower one with younger girls, and less interesting work. I am not unreasonable. I shall not expect miracles; do your best, and we'll help you on. I think you had better have a special coach to whom you can apply if you want help or explanation in your preparation. Now which of you girls would like to be Dreda's coach, and spare her a little time when it is needed?"

There was a simultaneous rustle of assent, but two voices spoke first, breaking the silence at identically the same moment.

"I!" cried Susan.

"Me!" cried Nancy.

Miss Drake smiled. "Oh, Nancy, Nancy!" she cried gaily; "a nice person *you* would be to coach another! Better give a little more attention to your own grammar, my dear. Very well, Susan, that is settled. You shall be Dreda's coach!"

Dreda and Susan looked at each other across the table in silence. Susan saw flushed cheeks and eyes suspiciously bright. Dreda stared in amazement, asking herself how it could be that anyone so much like the two elder sisters could at the same time be so diametrically different. Mary and Agnes were unusually plain, heavy-looking girls, but in Susan's face there was at this moment, a light of sympathy which made it strangely attractive. She possessed the family features, the family eyes, but Nature had evidently been prejudiced on her behalf and had given with a more generous hand. An extra shade of darkness on the eyebrows, an extra dip to the nose, a tiny curl to the lips, a tilt of the chin—these were trifles in themselves, but what an amazing improvement when taken in bulk! Dreda gazed and gazed, and as she did so there came to her one of those delightful experiences which most of us encounter once or twice as we go through life. As she met this strange girl's glance, a thrill of recognition ran through her veins; a voice in her heart cried, "*My Friend!*" and she knew just as surely as if she had been told in words that at the same moment Susan's heart had sounded the same glad welcome.

She said: "Thank you, Susan," in a voice unusually subdued, and bit her lips to keep back the tears.

Chapter Nine.

At twelve o'clock work was laid aside and Miss Drake accompanied the girls for an hour's constitutional. She claimed Dreda for her companion for the first part of the walk, for she had noticed the girl's humiliation, and was anxious to have a few words with her in private.

"I am sorry that you should have had such a disagreeable cross-questioning this morning, Dreda," she began brightly, "but I am sure you will realise that it was necessary. I was obliged to find out what you had been doing before I could make plans for the future. Now that is over, and we can move ahead. You will enjoy working with Susan. She is appreciative and thoughtful—a little slow in taking things in, perhaps, but for the present that will be a good thing, as it will make it all the easier for a quick girl like yourself to catch up to her in class work." Dreda glanced up sharply.

"I! Quick! How do you know?"

Miss Drake smiled mischievously.

"Oh, very easily—very easily, indeed! I am accustomed to work among girls, and when I get a new pupil I know at once under which category she will fall. When I saw you I said to myself—'Quick, ambitious, versatile!' I have no fear that you will fail to do anything to which you persistently give your mind."

"Ah!" groaned Dreda tragically, "but that's just what I can never do. For a little time—yes! I'm a *wonder* to work when I first get a craze. But—it passes! I get—*bored!* I've never stuck persistently to one thing in my life. The boys call me 'Etheldreda the Ready,' because I'm always bubbling over with enthusiasm at the beginning, and willing to promise any mortal thing you like—and then,"—she snapped her fingers in illustration—"Snap! the balloon bursts, and I collapse into nothing. It will be the same thing with lessons!"

Miss Drake held up her hand imperatively.

"Stop!" she cried clearly. "Stop! Never say that again, never *allow* yourself to say it. You know your failing in your own heart, and that is enough! Every time that you put it into words, and talk about it to others, gives it added strength and power and makes it more difficult to fight. My dear girl, you are not a child—how feeble to take for granted that you are going to continue in your old baby failings! Take for granted instead that you are going to live them down, and trample them beneath your feet. You'll have to fight for it, and to fight hard, but it will do you more good than any lessons I can teach. That's the best education, isn't it, to achieve the mastery over ourselves?"

Now, if meek Miss Bruce had delivered herself of similar sentiments, Dreda would have tilted her chin and wriggled contemptuously in her chair, muttering concerning "preaching," and wishing to goodness that the tiresome old thing would stop talking and get on with her work, but Miss Drake wore such a young and gallant air, as she strode along the country lane with her head thrown back, and her uplifted hand waving aloft, that the girl's ardent nature took flame; she tilted her own head, waved her own arm, and felt a tingling of martial zeal. Yes, she would work! Yes, she would fight! She would tread her enemies under foot and emerge from the conflict victorious, untrammelled, a paragon of virtues. She turned a dazzling smile upon her companion and heaved an ardent sigh.

"How beautifully you talk! Our old governess was so different! She did not understand my nature. I have wonderful ambitions, but I am so sensitive that I can't work against difficulties. I need constant encouragement and appreciation. A sensitive plant—"

"Oh, Dreda, please spare me that worn-out simile! Not work against difficulties, indeed! What nonsense you talk! It is not work at all when everything is easy and smooth. Don't deceive yourself, my dear—you are going to find plenty of difficulties, and to find them quickly, too. This very afternoon they will begin, when you tackle the new subjects and realise your own ignorance. You won't enjoy being behind your companions."

Dreda threw out her arms with a gesture of despair, but she made no further protest. Difficulties arising in the dim future she felt herself able to face resolutely enough, but the thought that they might begin that very afternoon dispelled her ardour. She listened to Miss Drake's further utterances with so quelled and dispirited an air that that quick-sighted lady felt that enough had been said for the moment, and calling her elder pupils to her side, set the two younger girls free to walk together.

51

It was the moment for which both had been longing, but a mutual shyness held them tongue-tied for the first hundred yards. Naturally it was Dreda who broke the silence.

"It was ripping of you to offer to coach me. I don't believe in learning all those things, but if I must, I must, and it would have been difficult all alone. I hope you don't mind."

"I want to," said Susan simply. "I've always wanted to do something for you, since the first time we met. It was at a Christmas party at the Rectory and you wore a black frock. I never thought then that you would come to school with us, but I wished you could be my friend. When I've made castles in the air they have always been about you, and something we could do together. I sat beside you at supper. Do you remember?"

No! Dreda had no recollection of the kind. She and her brothers and sisters had always cherished a secret contempt for the Webster sisters and had sedulously avoided them on every occasion. If Susan had been seated on one side at supper, it followed as a matter of course that Dreda herself had devoted her attention exclusively to whoever sat at the other side. She felt a faint pricking of conscience, and answered tentatively: "It is so long ago. I have a wretched memory. I remember we had lovely crackers at supper— but that's all. How did you come to notice me?"

"Because you were so pretty," Susan said. "Your sister is pretty too, very pretty, but she does not look so gay. And your brothers—they are such big, handsome boys. You are all handsome, and big, and strong, and have such romantic names. You seemed far more like a family in a book than real, live people. The 'Story-Book Saxons'—that was always our name for you when we spoke of you between ourselves. Do you think it is nice?"

"Very nice, indeed. 'Story-Book Saxons!' I must tell Rowena that." Dreda preened her head complacently. This simple admiration was most refreshing after the humiliations of the morning. "Perhaps we *are* rather unusual," she allowed. "Rowena is beautiful when she is in a good temper, and the boys are always bringing home prizes, and being captains in their sports. Maud is stupid, but she has lovely hair, and I, I'm not advanced in lessons—*your* sort of lessons—but Miss Bruce says I have a very original mind. When I'm grown up I don't intend to stodge along in the dull, humdrum fashion most women do. I mean to Do something. To Be something. To live for an Aim!"

Susan regarded her with serious eyes.

"What sort of aim?"

"Oh–h"—Dreda waved her arms with a sweeping movement—"I've not decided. There's plenty of time. But I mean to have a Career, and make my name known in the world."

"Don't you think," Susan asked tentatively, "that it is best to have a definite aim and to prepare for it beforehand?"

"You talk as if you had an ambition yourself!"

"I have!" said Susan quietly.

"You mean to be celebrated like me?"

"I am going to be an author. I hope I shall be celebrated. I shall try my best, but only time can show how I shall succeed."

"An author!" Dreda repeated disapprovingly. "*You!* How very odd! I have thought of being an author myself, and we are so different. I believe I could make up a very good story if I'd time. The only difficult part would be writing it out. Fancy perhaps fifty chapters! You'd get sick of them before you were half through, and have writers' cramp, and all sorts of horriblenesses. We might collaborate, Susan!"

Susan smiled, but showed no sign of weakening.

"I don't think that would do. We should never agree about what we wanted to say, but it would be delightful to read our stories aloud to each other, and discuss them together. The first heroine I make shall be exactly like you!"

"That's sweet of you. Begin at once—do! and read each chapter as it's done."

Susan's smile was somewhat wistful. She looked in Dreda's face with anxious eyes, as though waiting for a promise which must surely come, but Dreda remained blankly unresponsive. It never occurred to her for a moment that it could be possible to make a heroine out of Susan Webster!

Chapter Ten.

West End School was conducted on lines differing somewhat both from those of the modern public school and the old polite finishing seminary for young ladies. It accommodated in all about fifty pupils, and although games and examinations formed important parts of the curriculum, they were not regarded as being of such absorbing importance as in many modern schools. Miss Bretherton was a woman of lofty aims, who was continually looking beyond her pupils' schooldays to the time when they should be the women of Britain; the wives and mothers, and sisters and friends of the men who were to carry on the work of our great Empire, and who, humanly speaking, would do that work well or ill according to the manner in which their womankind influenced their lives. Miss Bretherton realised that the chief result of school study was not the mere storing of information, but the training of the brain to grapple with the great problems of life. Lessons were only means to an end. Half of that which was learnt with such pains would be forgotten before a dozen years had passed by; but the deeper lessons of industry, patience, self-restraint, would remain as habits of daily life. Formation of character—that was the one absorbing object which the Head held in view, and which underlay every scheme and arrangement. Miss Bretherton's manner was so staid, her nature so reserved, that her pupils were apt to credit her with being dull and easily deceived, little guessing that those quiet eyes were as searchlights turned upon their little foibles and vanities. During Dreda's first week at school her mood was pretty equally divided between enjoyment and misery. She loved the big, full, bustling house, the constant companionship of her kind, the chats over the study fire, the games in the playground; in a lesser degree she enjoyed the lessons also—those, at least, in which she was fairly proficient—and found Miss Drake a most interesting and inspiring teacher. She loved the interest which she excited, the flattering remarks of other girls, the quiet devotion of Susan; but she hated the rules of "early to bed and early to rise"; found it a penance to be obliged to practise scales, with icy fingers, for forty minutes before breakfast; was fretted and humiliated by her ignorance on many important subjects, and at the end of the long day often found herself tired, disappointed, and—hungry!

There is no doubt that a school menu is a distinct trial to the girl fresh from home. The girl accustomed to mix cream in a cup of freshly roasted, freshly ground coffee takes badly to the weak, groundy liquid so often supplied in its place. She grows tired to death of beef, mutton, and resurrection pie, and is inclined to declare that if the only way to become strong is to consume everlasting suet puddings, why, then, as a choice of evils, she prefers to be weak!

"Is it always as bad as this?" Dreda demanded plaintively of her room-mates as they brushed their locks in company before retiring to bed on the evening of her fifth day at West House. "Do you *never* have anything nice and light, that doesn't taste of suet and oven? Does it get better as summer comes on?"

"Worse!" pronounced Nancy shortly.

Dreda had devoted five whole days to the study of Nancy's character, and to this hour could not make up her mind whether she most liked or detested her. She was the oddest of girls: nothing seemed to excite her, nothing to trouble, nothing to please. Occasionally she would show swift, kindly impulses, as when she had offered to become Dreda's coach; but not a flicker of disappointment did she portray if such impulses were repulsed, not a gleam of pleasure if they were accepted. At other times she seemed to take a perverse pleasure in making the worst of a situation and playing the part of Job's comforter.

"Worse!" she sighed. "Much worse! Because it's warm weather, and your fancy lightly turns to nicer things. It's a bit of a cross to see strawberries in the shop windows, and them come home to 'Brother, where art thou?'"

"What brother?"

"Raisins!" said Nancy, and sighed again. "They lose each other in such steppes of suet."

Conscientious Susan exclaimed in protest.

"Nancy! Too bad. There is always stewed rhubarb!"

But this was poor comfort, for Dreda disliked stewed rhubarb almost as much as suet itself. She pouted disconsolately for several moments, then smiled with sudden inspiration.

"I'll get a doctor's order!"

"What for?"

"Plenty of fresh ripe fruit. Vegetarian diet. Fruit, and cream, and eggs during the summer heat!"

"How will you manage to get it?"

"I'll have something... I'll ask Rowena what's the best complaint: headaches or dizziness, or feeling tired. I'll tell mother it's the heavy food, and mother'll tell him, and he'll write to Miss Bretherton. I shall eat strawberries, and watch you search for 'brothers.'"

Nancy stared solemnly with her long, dark eyes.

"There was a girl here who tried that before—Netta Bryce. That very same dodge."

"Well?"

"She wished she hadn't."

"Why?"

"Try, and you'll find out."

"Nancy, you *are* horrid. What happened to her? Where is she now?"

"Dead!" croaked Nancy, and drew the screen around her bed. After that Dreda might question as much as she liked, but she knew well that never a reply would Nancy vouchsafe. It was really most tiresome!

She lay awake for a good ten minutes pondering over what *could* have happened to Netta Bryce, and if she had died soon, and under what conditions. Nancy was really the most aggravating of creatures!

Besides Miss Drake, commonly called "The Duck," there were two other resident teachers at West Hill. Mademoiselle—a tiny, pathetic-looking little creature, warranted to fly into a temper in a shorter time, and upon less provocation, than any other woman in the United Kingdom; and Fraulein, a lumpish but amiable creature who gave lessons in German and music. Miss Bretherton herself took the whole school for the morning Bible lesson, and had a disagreeable habit of descending upon the different forms at unexpected moments, and taking the place of the regular teacher. Of course, the surprise visit invariably happened just at the moment when the girls had "slacked," whereupon fright being added to ignorance, they would make such a poor display that they themselves were covered with confusion and their instructor with mortification. Almost every day at dinner time two or three girls could be observed with crimson cheeks and watery eyes gazing miserably at their plates, when the beholders would nudge each other significantly, and exchange glances of commiserating understanding. "Our turn next!"

Two masters also visited the school. Mr Broun, the professor of music, was a small, shaggy-looking personage, with a bumpy brow and eyes set extraordinarily far apart. He was a born musician, and, as a consequence, found it infinitely irritating to the nerves to be obliged to teach young ladies who had not one note of music in their composition, but whose parents considered an acquaintance with the pianoforte to be a necessity of education. When one of these unfortunates went up for her lesson, shouts and groans of despair could be heard outside the door of the music-room, accompanied by the sound of heavy footsteps pacing helplessly to and fro, and at the end of the half-hour the victim would emerge, red and tearful, or red and defiant, as her nature was, to recount gruesome stories of brutality to her companions. "He rapped my ringers with his pencil. I won't stand it. I'm sixteen. I'll write home and complain." Sandwiched in among the poor pupils were one or two who possessed real musical ability—Nancy, for instance, whose supple fingers seemed to draw mysterious sweetness and depths from the keys of the well-worn piano—and in these cases the lesson would extend far beyond its legitimate length and would take upon itself something of the nature of a recital, as Mr Broun himself took possession of the piano stool, to illustrate the effect which he wished produced. Then the girls in adjoining rooms would find their attention wandering from their books, and little groups "changing form" would linger outside the door listening with bated breath. Ah! if one could only play like *that*!

Mr Minns, the mathematical master, was built on wires, and expected one rapid explanation of the most complex rule to make it clear as crystal. After twenty years spent in teaching, he *still* professed to be prostrated with horror at each fresh exhibition of feminine obtuseness, and would groan, and writhe, and push his fingers through his hair, until it stood up round his head like a halo. He was Dreda's special *bête noire*, for, like many girls who excel in literature and composition, she detested the sight of a sum and had never grown beyond the stage of counting on her fingers beneath the table. If it had not been for Susan's laboriously patient explanations, nothing could have saved her from the most hopeless humiliation; but Susan had a gift of apt and fitting words, and of inventing illustrations which showed daylight through the thickest mist.

She rose early and worked late in order to have time to spare for her duties as coach, and Dreda was lavish in gratitude.

"You really *are* a saint! What should I do without you? Expire of pure misery and despair. As it is, I'm dying of overwork. I've a buzzy muzzy feeling in my brain which must mean something bad. Softening, I believe. It *does* come on from overstrain!"

Susan would smile, her quietly humorous smile, at these exaggerated statements, refusing to feel any anxiety about the health of such a blooming invalid.

Apart from arithmetic, however, Dreda made wonderful progress in her studies. Her native quickness of wits stood her in good stead; she learnt easily, and seized nimbly on salient points, so that, though her knowledge was superficial, she was always ready with an answer, and could enlarge so cleverly on what she *did* know, that the gaps of ignorance remained unsuspected. Susan, the prudent, shook her head over this juggling with fate, and foretold confusion in the coming examinations; but Dreda was content to sun herself in the present atmosphere of approbation and leave the future to take care of itself. Given a free hand by her parents, she had entered her name for every examination on the school list, and hardly a day passed that she did not propose a new scheme or exploit to her companions.

The time for these propositions was generally the cherished half-hour after tea, when the fourth form girls gathered round the fire in the study to chat over the doings and happenings of the day. Then Dreda was in her element, and every day, as it seemed, was filled with a fresh ambition.

"When does your school magazine come out next?"

"Never! Haven't got one to 'come out.'"

"*Haven't got one*? A school without a magazine! How disgraceful! I should be ashamed to confess it. Why haven't you?"

"Too much fag!"

Dreda gasped with horror.

"Why, even at home, where we are only six, we have an—an—" She paused, anxiously searching for a word which should be sufficiently vague— "an *annual*, with stories, and illustrations, and correspondence columns just like real. I was 'Aunt Nelly' and answered the questions. Such sport! ... 'Yes, my dear, at fifteen you are certainly far too young to be secretly engaged. Confide the whole story to your dear mother. A mother is ever a young girl's wisest confidante.'—(Of course, no one really asked me that. I made it up. You have to make up to fill the page.) ... 'So sorry your complexion is spotty. Rub it over with lemon juice and oil. Never mind if you *are* ugly. Be good, and you'll get a sweet expression, and that is better than any beauty.' ... Ha, ha!" She tossed her golden mane with a derisive laugh. "*Just* like a real mag.! Then I put things in for the boys, of course— got them out of cricket reports and encyclopaedias—it looks out well to have learned bits here and there. And you can give lovely hints! It would be awfully useful in a school, because you could say whatever you wanted without being personal ... 'No! the old adage, "Finding is keeping" does *not* apply to your companions' indiarubbers and pencils. It is not considered honourable in good society to pare off initials inscribed thereon for purposes of identification.'" She chuckled happily. "Don't I do it well? I really *have* the knack! ... I can't think why you don't have one."

"How should we find the time?" queried Susan earnestly. "First to compose the things—and then write them out neatly would take hours and hours."

"I would write them out. It looks ever so much better if it's all in one handwriting."

The girls exchanged glances. Dreda certainly wrote a very legible hand, but they were already beginning to feel a trifle dubious about her ready promises.

"My dear, it would take *years*! You would never get through. Only yesterday you were preparing us for softening of the brain from overwork. You really must curb this overflowing energy." Nancy narrowed her eyes in her most fascinating smile, in which still lurked a spice of derision. "Your welfare is very precious to us; we can't afford to risk it for the sake of a magazine!"

Dreda flushed, and wriggled impatiently on her seat. She never could tell whether Nancy was in fun or in earnest.

"I am not proposing to take on more work. It would be a distraction!" she declared loftily. "I love making up stories and poetry, and reading what other people have written. I'd get up early, and do it in play hours. It would be a labour of love. Besides, it would cultivate our style. 'The Duck' is literary herself. I dare say she'd let it count as composition!"

The girls brightened visibly at this suggestion. It would be distinctly more amusing to write for their own magazine than to cudgel their brains to produce a sheet full of ideas on the abstruse subjects suggested by Miss Drake. They edged a little nearer the fire, straightened their backs, and fell to discussion.

"Perhaps she might."

"We'll ask her."

"She might be editor."

"She could write a lovely story herself."

"Bertha could illustrate. She draws the killingest pictures. There was one of the fifth dormitory at 6 a.m. You saw all the girls asleep, and their heads were killing. Amy had a top-knot that had fallen on one side, Phyllis a pigtail about two inches long, and as thin as a string. You know her miserable little wisp of hair. Mary was lying on her back with her mouth wide open. It was the image of her. She's nearly as good as Hilda Cowham. We might call her 'Hilda Cowman' as a *nom de plume*. Wouldn't it look professional?"

Dreda was a trifle annoyed that the position of editor had not been offered to herself as the originator of the movement, and she likewise cherished the belief that she was entitled to take a prominent place as illustrator; but she consoled herself with the reflection that when the magazine was really started her previous experience could not fail to be useful.

"We'll have stories, and essays, and poetry, and competitions, and advertisements at the end. You have to pay for advertisements, and that pays for stationery."

"What sort of advertisements?"

"Every sort. Exchanging stamps and post cards, selling snapshots—anything you like. I should put: 'Fifth form pupil will coach junior for ten minutes daily in exchange for fagging: hot water, sewing on buttons, darning, etcetera.' I'm not used to mending. It's the limit! What shall we call it?"

"The magazine? *The Grey House Monthly—Messenger—Herald*—something of that kind. We ought to bring in the name of the school."

"I don't see why. I think it would be nicer without. Less amateury. The—*Casket*. Wouldn't *Casket* be good? It implies that it is full of treasures."

"*The Torch*! That's nicer than *Casket*, and sounds more spirited. We could have a picture of a woman holding up a lamp, with the word 'Progress' written across the beams—like they do in the *Punch* cartoons. I think *Torch* would be lovely."

"Why not *Comet*?" asked Nancy in her brief, quiet tones, narrowing the double line of black eyelashes as she spoke so as to hide the expression of her eyes.

There was a moment's pause, broken by Dreda's quick, suspicious question:

"Why *Comet*?"

"Why not?"

"Do you mean because of the *tail*?"

"Comets *do* have tails, don't they? So do magazines!"

That was all very well, but the silence which followed the explanation showed that suspicion still rankled. Dreda arched her eyebrows at Barbara, who shrugged in reply. Susan wrinkled her brows, and Norah pursed her lips. What was Nancy really thinking inside that sleek, well-shaped little head? Comets appeared suddenly; remained to be a ten days' talk and wonder, and then—mysteriously disappeared! Instinctively Dreda stiffened her back, and registered an inward vow that she would spare neither time nor pains to make the magazine a permanent and shining light!

Chapter Eleven.

To the delight of Dreda, and the more subdued satisfaction of the other pupils, a magazine received the sanction of the headmistress and Miss Drake, provided that it did not aim at more than a quarterly appearance.

"It will waken you up!" said the latter, smiling whimsically at her pupils. "You are all rather apt to go to sleep at times, especially when a little originality is desired; but remember that the magazine receives official sanction as a means of education, not as a receptacle for any rubbish you may choose to scribble. We'll have stories, of course; but I have suffered under stories in other amateur magazines, and am determined to raise ours above the usual level. Every girl who wishes to write a story must draw out a synopsis of the plot and submit it to me before she embarks on the task of writing it out. I will then refuse or accept it, and in the latter case will talk it over with the author, giving her some hints as to arrangement, treatment of points, which will, I hope, be of value to the story. In fact, I should like to have the entire synopsis of the magazine drawn up and brought to me a month before publication. So what a Tartar of an editor I am going to be! I have quite decided that if I am to get through the work at all, I must have an understudy, a sub-editor, so to speak, who can keep the contributors up to time, collect their suggestions, and submit them for my criticism. It will involve a good deal of steady, methodical work. I wonder—"

"I'll do it, Miss Drake. Let me. I offered to be editor before."

The words leaped from Etheldreda's lips before Miss Drake's eyes had wandered halfway round the class. Mary's face wore its usual blank stare, Barbara sniggled with obvious contempt, Nancy veiled her eyes with her thick, dark lashes, Susan flushed suddenly a brilliant red.

Both Miss Drake and Dreda herself were arrested by the sight of those flaming cheeks, for Susan was, as a rule, so calm and self-restrained that any exhibition of excitement on her part was bound to attract attention. What was the matter? Why did she look so anxious and eager? What were the words which seemed trembling on her lips? Dreda felt complacently convinced that as her own friend and ally Susan was longing to champion her cause. Miss Drake smiled and asked encouragingly:

"Well, Susan, what is it? What were you going to say?"

The red mounted higher and higher until it reached the roots of the tightly brushed hair. Susan's very ears seemed aflame, and her voice had the husky note of repressed excitement.

"I—I was going to offer—I thought I could do the work for you, Miss Drake."

Etheldreda's gasp of dismay was heard throughout the room. Her cheeks rivalled Susan's in their flame of indignation. *Susan* to play her false, to endeavour to wrest a coveted place from a friend! Susan an enemy, a rival! Dreda felt a vehement, overwhelming disgust for the whole universe and its inhabitants, a shattering of faith in every cherished ideal! Never, no never again, could she bring herself to believe in a human creature!

The two girls sat silent, awaiting the mistress's decree, and Miss Drake looked slowly from one flushed face to the other, her usually smooth forehead showing two deep horizontal lines. It was her "thinking look"—the look which she wore when she was trying to explain an unusually difficult point in the day's lessons. The girls watched her anxiously, saw the lines clear away, and the light of decision drawn in her eyes; wondered if it were in imagination only that at the same time they caught the sound of a faint sigh of regret.

"Thank you, girls," she said slowly. "It is sweet of you both to be so ready to help. I am ever so much obliged to you, Susan—but Dreda spoke first. I think I will decide to give the post to her."

Nobody heard any more than this, though Miss Drake continued talking for several moments. Dreda was thrilling from head to foot with triumphant joy. Susan's flush had deepened from crimson to an absolute magenta. The other girls were torn between sympathy and amazement! For once in their lives they were unanimous in condemnation of the beloved Duck's judgment, and could not imagine what she had been dreaming about to choose Dreda Saxon for a post of responsibility, when that most reliable of Susans could have been had for the asking. No one made any remark, however, and Dreda, glancing expectantly around, failed to meet any of the congratulatory smiles which were surely her right on so auspicious an occasion. The girls were sitting stiff and straight in their seats, staring at their desks in their most prim and wooden manner. Susan was the only one who ventured a struggling smile, and from her Dreda contemptuously turned aside. Hypocrisy was a failing for which she had no tolerance!

It was with a visible effort that Miss Drake continued the discussion in her usual bright, cheery manner.

"The term is already a month old. I should like to have the synopsis of the contents of the magazine by to-day fortnight—say the tenth of next month. We can then allow three weeks for composition and a week for typing, and still have the magazine ready a week before the holidays. I have quite decided that everything must be typed: the effect, as a whole, will be far better. Faults in style and composition stand out before us in print as they never do in our own familiar handwriting. Moreover, I have other schemes working in my head." She paused, smiling mysteriously. "I won't explain now, but later on, perhaps ... Do your best, girls! Some of you have real talent. Who knows, this little venture may be the beginning of some great career. How proud I should be in time to come if I could say of a celebrated author: 'She was my pupil. She wrote her first story or essay or poem for our school magazine!'"

She paused, looking round the class. Once more her gaze lingered on Susan's downcast face, but there was no response in its immovable lines. The other girls vouchsafed strained, uneasy smiles. Only from Dreda's ecstatic eyes there flashed back a joyful comprehension. How beautiful the girl looked! Her vivid colouring, all pink, and white, and gold, made an almost startling contrast to the duller tints of the other girls.

It was impossible to resist the fascination of so fair a sight, yet there was a touch of wistfulness in the teacher's smile.

The class dismissed, it was time to go upstairs to dress for supper, and Dreda found herself alone in the bedroom with her two companions. Nancy peeled off her blouse, threw it upon the bed, and brushed out her heavy locks in determined silence. Susan approached Dreda with a tremulous smile.

"Oh, Dreda—I'm glad! I hope the magazine will be a success. If I can help you in any way do let me try."

But Dreda glared at her with sparkling eyes.

"You are *not* glad! You tried your very best to be editor yourself, though you *knew* how disappointed I should be. I thought you were my friend. You are not. You are an enemy, and not even an honest enemy at that! You need not trouble yourself about me any more, for lessons or anything else. I can get on quite well alone!"

Susan shrank, as if from a blow.

"Dreda, you are angry. You don't understand. It's no trouble. I love to help you."

"Much obliged. I don't care for such help. Please don't talk to me any more. I *am* angry. I have a right to be angry!"

Dreda pulled her screen with a jerk, cutting herself off from the corner where Susan performed her toilet. Seated on her bed, Nancy brushed at her long, sleek hair, keeping it spread as a veil before her face. Dreda waited in vain for a glance of sympathy, or understanding, but it never came, even when Susan had crept softly from the room and the constraint of her presence was removed. Nancy finished brushing her hair, and rose to her feet in the lightest, most unperturbed of fashions:

"Got any pins you can spare?"

Nancy was celebrated for the number of pins which she used in her toilet. Things wouldn't fasten without them, she declared. She was fairly bristling with pins, so that her most ardent adorers moderated their embraces, mindful of the scratches which had been their reward in days of inexperience. Dreda eagerly selected half a dozen of her most cherished fancy-headed pins, and handed them across the bed.

"Of course. As many as you like. I say, Nance, I'm sorry to have made a scene. I *could not* help it!"

"Oh, don't apologise. I like a good row now and then. Not for myself—it's too much trouble—but it's amusing to listen to other people when they get excited. They give themselves away so delightfully."

Dreda flushed, and knitted her brows.

"I wasn't at all excited in this case. I was angry—*righteously* angry! It's one's duty to protest against mean, underhand actions."

"Such as wanting the best positions for ourselves?"

"Certainly not. That is only natural ambition—laudable ambition. The mean thing is to try to oust someone else—your own best friend, when you know she could do it better than you!"

"Yes!" mused Nancy thoughtfully. "That does sound mean ... This sub-editor post is going to be so difficult that it ought certainly to go to the right person. A careful, methodical, machine-like sort of creature, who will never forget or let others forget. The girls are slack enough about regular work, and will be a hundred times worse about an extra, and The Duck is a tartar about punctuality. It's going to be a problem to please them and 'keep the peace.' But you have had a magazine at home, so you know all about it. Susan has had no experience."

Nancy had seated herself on her bed once more, her hands clasped round her knees, her lips slightly apart, showing a glimpse of the golden bar round the front teeth; her long, Eastern-looking eyes met Dreda's without a blink, yet for some mysterious reason Dreda felt her cheeks flush and a jarring doubt awoke in her mind. "A machine"—"never forgetting—never late!" Not even her youthful complaisance could apply that description to herself. The ghosts of past enterprises seemed to rear reproachful heads, reminding her of their existence. To each of the number had been sworn eternal fidelity, yet how short had been their lives! The factory girl, for instance, who had received three long, enthusiastic letters, and after the lapse of a year was still awaiting the receipt of the fourth. Poor Emma Larkins had been so appreciative and grateful. Dreda had been able to talk of nothing else for the first week of the correspondence. She had planned a lifelong friendship, and in imagination had seen herself, aged and wealthy, acting the gracious benefactress to a second generation. *How* had she happened to forget? She had been busy, her father had taken her for a trip abroad, she had joined a society for the study of French classics. The time had flown by until she had been ashamed to begin writing again. No doubt another correspondent had taken her place ... "*Susan has no experience.*" True! Yet if one wished to describe Susan's character, could one do it more aptly than by using Nancy's own words? "Careful, methodical, machine-like as to accuracy!" *What* did Nancy mean? Was she really and truly in earnest, or did some hidden meaning lurk behind the seemingly innocent words? Dreda drew a long breath, and set her teeth in the determination to set an example of diligence and punctuality to all sub-editors beneath the sun, and by so doing to demonstrate in the most practical of fashions her suitability for the post.

Chapter Twelve.

All work and no play makes Jack a dull boy—and Jill a dull girl also. Miss Bretherton was a firm believer in this old adage, and loyally tried to provide a due proportion of amusement for her pupils. In the winter terms bad weather often interfered with outdoor sports, but every alternate Saturday evening a reception was held in the drawing-room between the hours of seven and nine thirty, on which occasions thirty pupils dressed for the fray with gleeful anticipation, and the thirty-first with trembling foreboding, for it was she who was chosen to play the part of hostess and take sole management and responsibility of the entertainment.

All pupils in the fourth and fifth term were considered old enough to be hostesses, so that no girl was called upon to play the part more than twice a year; but when the great occasions arrived, ambition mingled with nervousness, and the heroine of the hour, calling to mind the errors and failings of her companions, determined to profit by them, and achieve a brilliant success for herself.

The duties of the hostess were sufficiently onerous. She was responsible for the arrangement of flowers in the drawing-room, could distribute chairs and sofas as she thought fit, and punctually at seven o'clock must be on duty prepared to receive her guests and direct the passing round of tea and coffee. The first hour was dedicated to conversation; for the second, some form of amusement must be designed and arranged, and lastly, a sum of ten shillings had to be so expended as to provide some form of light refreshment which should be consumed before the company dispersed.

To take the last duty first, ten shillings divided into thirty portions (the younger pupils were not allowed to stay up for "supper") did not allow a very handsome sum per head! Most hostesses came down and down in their ambition until they reached the ignominious level of lemonade and buns, but there had been occasional daring flights of fancy, as when Nancy had provided thirty large sausage rolls, and the poor sufferers whose digestions forbade playing with such dainties last thing at night found no choice offered to them, and were obliged to retire to bed hungry and wrathful. An hour's amusement was also somewhat difficult to arrange, as nothing short of an official decree would induce a music pupil to perform in public, a singer to sing, or an elocutionist to give a recital. Paper games and competitions of a somewhat feeble nature were the general refuge of the destitute, though each hostess started out with the determination of hitting on something more amusing and exciting. No difficulty as to amusement or provision, however, could compare for one moment with the ordeal of that first hour, that hour of reception and conversation, the horrors of which each fresh hostess seemed to find more onerous than the last. To sail forward and shake hands with Miss Bretherton in her best grey silk, to welcome her to her own drawing-room, and engage in light conversation about the weather—could one imagine a more paralysing ordeal? Then no sooner was the Head disposed of in one arm-chair, than in would come a party of your best friends, all primed with mischievous determination to make you giggle, and so reduce you to humiliation. While one was elegantly shaking hands, a second was furtively pulling hideous grimaces, a third was pinching your arm, and a fourth treading on your toe. Crimson-faced and quivering, you would convey these last arrivals across the room and introduce them to Miss Bretherton, for it was one of the tiresome rules that no one guest was supposed to know another at the moment of entering these social gatherings. Thick and fast they came at last, and more and more and more, all needing to be welcomed with appropriate words, conducted to seats, introduced, provided with tea. The poor hostess had no time to think of herself, and her worst moments began when all her guests had assembled, for then she must perforce watch for the moment when conversation became forced and fitful and promptly move the pawns about the board, introducing them to fresh pawns, lingering until conversation was safely afloat! The members of the staff never deigned to help the poor struggling novice in the art of entertainment; it was darkly suspected that they rather added to her difficulties by adopting haughty, reserved airs which called for greater displays of generalship. With what a sigh of relief was the striking of eight o'clock greeted by the harassed mistress of the ceremonies!

Dreda Saxon's first experience as hostess arrived just about the middle of the term, and, unlike her companions, she was greatly elated at the prospect. No fears disturbed her night's rest; she received the half-sovereign for refreshments as gratefully as if it had been a fortune, and graciously "allowed" a few favoured friends to join the troupe of "dramatic impersonators" who were to provide the hour's amusement.

Everyone wanted to be a dramatic impersonator. It sounded much more exciting than sitting primly looking on beneath the eyes of the teaching staff; but Dreda had made a careful selection of Susan, Nancy, Barbara, and two lanky, overgrown third form sisters, Molly and Florry Reece, and sturdily refused to add to their number. Norah West in especial was much injured at being passed over, for she cherished a schoolgirl's adoration for the quiet Susan, and until Dreda's appearance on the scene had invariably been included in any scheme in which either she or Nancy were interested.

"I always did everything with everybody. I was always *in* everything until you came," she cried resentfully.

"Were you? Dear me! Then you should be glad of a rest," responded naughty Dreda, when, needless to say, Norah waxed more indignant than before.

"That Etheldreda Saxon is really getting insupportable," she announced to her companions at dinner on Saturday morning. "A new-comer and a fourth form girl, and she tries to boss the school. She's not a bit good at her work either, except at things she can make up out of her own head at a moment's notice. What right has she to give herself airs?" The companion shrugged her shoulders with disappointing indifference.

"I don't know. What does it matter? It pleases her, and it don't hurt us. She's good at hitting on new ideas anyhow, and that's a comfort. Dramatic impersonations sounds a lot better than paper games. I'm quite looking forward to to-night."

Now Norah had had paper games on a recent occasion when she had played the part of hostess, so she felt herself snubbed, and sulked for the whole afternoon, disdaining to take any notice of the whispering and laughing, the rushings to and fro, the wholesale confiscation of "properties," indulged in by Dreda and her troupe.

When the evening arrived she put on her second best dress, and purposely dallied until the very last moment before entering the drawing-room. She wished and expected to annoy Dreda by slighting her hospitality, but Dreda was too much absorbed in the excitement of the moment to remember past differences, so that the reluctant Norah found herself greeted with the most radiant of smiles, and was promptly escorted across the room and introduced to Mademoiselle in characteristic fashion.

"Mademoiselle, may I introduce my friend Miss West? Miss West is quite a distinguished example of our *jeune fille* sportive! I am sure you will like to know her. Miss West—Mademoiselle Saudre."

Mademoiselle chuckled with delight, and subdued splutterings of amusement sounded round the room while the *jeune fille* sportive took her seat with a very red face, miserably conscious that she was handicapped with a new nickname which would remain with her for the rest of her school life.

It was amusing to note the expression, half-approving, half-dismayed, with which Miss Bretherton watched the self-possessed young hostess. These evening At Homes had been instituted with the express design of preparing the elder pupils to be of social use to their mothers on their return home; to be able to make an introduction in due form, and to overcome awkward self-consciousness. It was a trifle disconcerting, however, to behold so very full-fledged a bantling, to find oneself treated with benevolent patronage, and to see the old rules set at naught in favour of startling innovations. Dreda had requisitioned two of the maids to take charge of the tea-table, and ordered their movements with the air of a commander-in-chief; she strolled about the room—taking part in the conversations of the different groups, and, when necessary, introducing new subjects with unblushing inconsequence.

As, for instance: "Yes; it has been terribly foggy. Quite the worst October on record. Have you ever been in Switzerland?"

The startled hearers were dumb for some moments, and then one of the number announced that she was going to Saint Moritz in January to take part in the winter sports, whereupon everyone was full of interest and curiosity, and Dreda swept onward to another bored-looking group, and hurled another conversational arrow.

At last—far sooner than usual, as everyone allowed—the clock struck eight, and immediately the two maids came forward, and, still under Dreda's superintendence, moved all the seats to the far end of the room, shutting off the portion by the door by means of three outstretched screens. The dramatic impersonations were about to begin!

73

A scene from English history formed the first item on the programme, and the screens being duly removed, an imposing figure was discerned strutting slowly to and fro, clad in a white bath gown on which a selection of shining dish-covers had been fastened with a very fair effect of armoury. Behind this imposing personage paced two other figures, cloaked and draped in would-be old-world fashion, who smirked as they went, and, bowing and scraping, pointed mysteriously to a green baize tablecloth stretched on the floor in mysteriously lumpy outline. The haughty person in the dish-covers waved aside these confidences with an air of impatience, then suddenly waxing wrathful, turned upon his companions and issued dumb but imperious commands. A chair was produced, and the attendants stood by in evident discomfort the while their seated master pointed his hand rebukingly towards the green patch on the floor. And then began a curious phenomenon, for the lumpy mass beneath the green tablecloth suddenly awoke to movement; a rhythmical, regular movement which swayed to and fro, up and down, creeping ever nearer and nearer to the seated monarch. When at length the edge of the cloth actually touched his august feet, horror and consternation were depicted on the faces of the attendants, while their master arose in leisurely dignity, and delivered in pantomime what was evidently a most instructive and admonitory address.

Hearty clapping and cries of "Canute! Canute!" from the stalls greeted the end of this performance, whereupon the green tablecloth was hastily thrown aside and the "waves" appeared in the persons of Molly and Florry, somewhat hot and red in the face as a result of their seclusion, but satisfied that their efforts had produced quite the most striking effect in the performance.

A bell rang. The screens were hastily pushed forward, and Barbara's fingers could be heard laboriously pounding out her latest "piece" on the piano, the while audible preparations were taking place for item number two. Barbara was not musical by nature, and in addition to a woodenness of touch, possessed a habit of playing the treble notes a distinct beat in advance of the bass, peculiarly exasperating to her instructress. Poor Fraulein! her expression suggested an attack of indigestion rather than an amused spectator of a dramatic entertainment!

Te-tum, te-tum, tum-tum! The last uncertain chords quavered to an end, the screens were again withdrawn, and the stage was discovered full of characters, dressed with some ingenuity to represent the principal personages in "Young Lochinvar." In arranging the *dramatis persona*some difficulty had arisen from the fact that none of the girls was willing to represent the elderly bridegroom so unflatteringly described as "a laggard in love and a dastard in war." It was not an ingratiating character, and Nancy and Barbara flatly refused to personate it. Susan could do it, she was the smallest, and would best look the part. For two minutes on end Susan stoutly refused to do anything of the kind, and then placidly consented, being of a peace-at-any-price disposition, which found it easier to submit than to preserve a determined opposition. She submitted, therefore, and reaped her reward in the shape of a costume which was beyond doubt the most striking in the group. A Norfolk jacket, a shawl pleated to represent a kilt, and a plaid thrown across her shoulders, were but insignificant details compared to the delight of sporting a pair of whiskers manufactured out of two long heads of pampas grass, so white, so silky, so bushy that they had really to be seen to be appreciated! The pampas grasses had been Dreda's inspiration, and when she had tied them securely into place, run several long black crayon marks from nose to chin, and popped a pair of spectacles over the eyes, behold the demure Susan transformed into so comical an imitation of an old man that the spectators rocked on their seats with merriment. There he stood, "plucking his bonnet and plume," while Dreda simpered in a corner, and Nancy as Lochinvar interviewed Barbara in the character of indignant father. Both actors had donned imitations of the Scottish costume, and the former made a picturesque figure as he led forward his lady love.

"One touch to her hand, and one word in her ears,

And they reached the hall door, and the charger stood near."

The charger was represented by an ancient and battered hobby horse, astride which the eloping lovers galloped violently across the stage, to disappear from sight through the open doorway. Confusion followed among the spectators, who hurriedly supplied themselves with imaginary steeds and galloped off in wild pursuit.

Again there was no difficulty in guessing the poem represented, but long and continued applause testified to the delight of the audience, while a special call was given to the wearer of the pampas whiskers.

After an interval of several minutes the screens were withdrawn for the third impersonation, when an impromptu bed was beheld placed on the extreme left of the stage. Lying snugly snoozled into a pillow was a fair head, at sight of which the audience laughed uproariously, for the head belonged to Dreda Saxon; but her fair hair, parted in the middle and plastered straightly down on either side, gave a ridiculously staid and old-world effect to her pink and white face. She snored gently, unperturbed by the mocking laughter, and presently two stout dames hurried into the room, and with a great show of agitation, roused the damsel from her sleep. Her arms were thrust into a blue dressing-gown, her bare feet into bedroom slippers, and, thus attired, she was escorted past a second screen into the presence of two grave and reverend segniors, who fell on their knees and humbly kissed her outstretched hand. The ludicrous solemnity of Dreda's face beneath the plastered bandeaux of hair brought down the house, and no one had the least difficulty in recognising in the representation the youthful Queen Victoria at the moment of her accession.

There was only enough time left for two more representations: Sir Walter Raleigh spreading his cloak on the ground so that Queen Elizabeth could escape the mud, and a spirited rendering of Horatius keeping the bridge, in which last representation Nancy won much applause as the "great Lord of Luna" clanking a four-fold shield in the shape of large-sized tea trays. The bridge was typified by a blackboard stretched between two tables—and the manner in which Horatius made his final dive into a nest of cushions was blood-curdling to behold. In truth, the hour's amusement passed like a flash, and when Dreda in ordinary dress re-entered the drawing-room at the head of her troupe, she was everywhere greeted with congratulations and applause.

"Supper" was another surprise, consisting, as it did, of fruit salad and whipped-up cream. The fortunates who were first in the field waxed eloquent in appreciation, but, alas! the cream soon fell short, and the last helpings of "salad" were so small as to be almost invisible.

"But some people are never satisfied," quoth Dreda scornfully. "What if the salad *did* run short! It was a feast of reason and a flow of soul. I've no pity for a person whose mind can't soar above stewed prunes!"

Chapter Thirteen.

The energy with which Etheldreda the Ready set about her work as sub-editor threatened to ruin the magazine before its birth, for intending contributors grew so tired of daily and sometimes hourly reminders that by the end of a week weariness had developed into right-down crossness and irritation. "For goodness' sake leave me alone. I'm sick of the name of the old magazine! If you worry me once more I won't do a thing—so there!" Such answers were more than a little disconcerting to one who had worked herself up to a white heat of enthusiasm, and could neither think, dream, nor speak of any other subject under the sun. So engrossed was Dreda in trying to keep other writers to the mark, that it was not until ten day's of the allotted fourteen had passed by that she set to work to think out her own contribution. It was to be a story, of course—not a stupid, amateury, namby-pamby story, such as you could read in other school magazines, but something striking and original, that would make everyone talk and wonder, and lie awake at night. So far so good; but when the time for writing it arrived it was astonishingly difficult to hit upon a suitable idea! Dreda chewed the end of her pen, wrote "Synopsis of Plot" at the top of her paper in an imposing round hand with the downstrokes elaborately inked, dotted wandering designs here and there, and cudgelled her brains for inspiration. There must be a girl, of course—a girl heroine, blonde and lovely, and an adventuress (brunette), and a hero. But she did not intend to write a love story—that was piffle. Something *really* thrilling and dangerous! She mentally ran over a list of misadventures—fire, flood, shipwreck. She had read of them all dozens of times over; and, mentioned in a synopsis, they would have quite an ordinary effect. It was after hours of anxious deliberation, during which ordinary lessons went completely to the wall, that the brilliant idea of an earthquake flashed upon Dreda's mind. An earthquake story might be as complicated as one pleased, for all the superfluous people could be killed off at the crucial moment, while legal papers and wills could disappear, so that one could not even be expected to unravel the mystery! She hovered uncertainly between three sensational titles—"A Hopeless Quest," "For Ever Hidden," "In the Twinkling of an Eye!"—and plunged boldly into the first sentence of the synopsis without having the faintest idea how it should end:

"A lovely young girl, Leila (English, yellow hair, sixteen) lives on a beautiful isle which had been a volcano hundreds of years before. (This will not be mentioned till the last, but mysterious remarks made about rumblings, to

77

prepare the mind.) Dolores (Spanish), aged seventeen, pretends to be her friend, but is really jealous. They stay together at a country house with a veranda, and exciting things happen. Leila is supposed to be an orphan, and Dolores patronises her because she is poor. An English officer comes to call, and staggers back at sight of Leila. (He is really her father.) Dolores makes mischief, and persuades him to leave her all his money. They go to the lawyers, and Leila goes out for a sail in a boat to cheer her spirits. While she is sailing, the volcano blows up and everyone is killed. Leila is picked up by a passing ship, and inherits the money."

Compared with this sensational programme, Susan's story promised to be deplorably tame and uneventful, and Dreda curled her lip in scorn as she read the neatly written lines:

"I want to write the story of a man who was naturally very nervous and afraid, but who hid it so well that everyone believed him to be a hero. I want to show that he really did become brave, because his friends believed in him, and he tried to be worthy of their trust."

"Gracious! How dull. It sounds like a tract. Susan is a dear; but she's a currant bun when all is said and done, and she can't get away from it. They *are* stodgers!" quoth Miss Dreda, with a shrug, as she placed the paper beside her own in her desk. Her anger against Susan had died a rapid death, for the double reason that she herself found it impossible to harbour resentment, and that Susan steadily refused to be a second party to a quarrel. Scornfully though her help had been refused, she offered it afresh every evening, and after three days' experience of struggle and defeat, Dreda was thankful to accept.

"But you *were* mean about the editorship, all the same. It wasn't like you, Susan!" she declared severely, feeling it would be too great a condescension to capitulate without protest. "You are generally quite sweet about helping other people. I don't understand what you were thinking about!"

Susan's quiet smile seemed to express agreement with this last statement, but she made no protest and allowed herself to be kissed and petted with a condescending "We'll say no more about it, will we, dear? Now for this exercise—it's a perfect brute!"

78

It was only by dint of ceaseless entreaties and cajoleries that the sub-editor succeeded in collecting a respectable number of entries for the first number of the magazine before the appointed date, and if the absolute truth had been known she was already feeling overweighted with the cares of office. It was a fag to be worried out of one's life, and as a result to be disliked rather than praised.

"I shake in my shoes at the very sight of Dreda Saxon!" said Norah West of the spectacles and freckles. "There's no peace in life while she is on the rampage. This school has never been the same since she came. She seems to have upset everything."

Nancy offered to contribute an article on "Characteristics of School Celebrities—Literary and Sportive," and refused to be coaxed to a more decorous subject. "That, or nothing!" was her mandate, so down it went on the synopsis, followed, by way of contrast, by Mary Webster's "Essay on Ancient Greece," and the head girl's "Great Women of History." Beryl Turner, who had a passion for figure drawing, unjustified by skill, submitted half a dozen sketches of an impossible young woman apparently entirely devoid of joints, to explain which she proposed to write a story, thus entirely reversing the usual process of illustration; and, fired by a desire to show her own artistic superiority, Dreda hastily embellished her own paper with two vignette paintings of her own heroines. Leila, with luxuriant locks of yellow, splashed with green, and Dolores with inky hair and eyes of a rich gamboge. On the afternoon of the fourteenth day of the month Dreda spent her recreation hour in arranging the collected sheets to the best advantage, and in fastening them within the cover of an old exercise book. She was aglow with self-satisfaction at having accomplished her task in time, and intended to lay special stress on the fact in her next letter home and so win from the home circle that admiration and praise which her schoolfellows were so slow to bestow.

On the whole, she was well pleased with the result of her labours, and looked forward with a lively curiosity to Miss Drake's comments and criticisms. When the booklet was finished and a printed label pasted in the middle of the black cover, she laid it carefully inside her desk and went to rejoin her companions by the study fire. They stopped talking as she approached, and began to "rag" in true school fashion.

"Here comes our literary friend. Quite worn out with the strain of her intellectual efforts! Sit down, my love, and calm your fevered brow!" This from Barbara, while Norah cried scornfully:

"Look at her fingers—inked to the joints! Anyone could tell she was a budding author!"

"Did you tie the papers together with blue ribbon? That's an absolute necessity. I have a piece I could give you."

"Thank you, Nancy. I'll accept it with pleasure—for my hair. The book is finished and needs no trimmings. It looks beautifully neat and professional. I can't show it to anyone until my—my colleague has seen it and made her alterations; but as soon as it comes back—"

She nodded in condescending fashion, and the girls chuckled and exchanged twinkling glances.

"'My colleague'! That's good!"

"Good word, Dreda! Bring that in in your story. It has a fine effect."

"I'm thankful it is finished at last. We shall be able to sleep in peace to-night without being disturbed by your plunging and snortings. I've always heard that geniuses were trying to live with, but they are even worse by night than by day!"

"At what time are you going to present the Opus to your colleague? After prep, to-morrow? Then I beg to suggest that until it has been reviewed and the verdict passed the subject shall be forbidden. The strain is *too* great!"

Norah rolled her eyes, a performance rendered weirdly effective by the presence of her large round glasses, and the other girls taking up the clue, flopped in their seats, leant feebly against a neighbouring shoulder, and fanned themselves faintly with their handkerchiefs. As a rule, Dreda was as quick to take offence as she was to forgive, but this afternoon she manifested no signs of irritation. "They laugh who win," and no one could deny that she had won this time—won all along the line—in gaining consent to the establishment of a magazine, in obtaining the post of sub-editor; lastly, and most striking of all, in being ready up to time, despite the gloomy prophecies to the contrary.

For the next twenty-four hours she was her brightest, most charming self, so radiant with happiness that she overflowed with sympathy and kindness to all around. She nursed little Vida Neale, the baby of the school, on her knee, and recounted such fascinating stories that earache was forgotten in squeals of delighted merriment. She went up early to dress for the evening and carried hot water to the cubicles of her four best friends; she talked in the most amiable of fashions to poor, dull Fraulein at supper; listened to remarks on the superiority of Germany with a self-control bordering on the miraculous; and finally laid her head down on the pillow of her bed with the feeling of being at peace with all the world.

"Prosperity suits me," she told herself, snuggling cosily beneath the clothes. "It brings out the best points in my disposition. I ought never to be crossed!"

The next morning passed slowly. Dreda did not distinguish herself at lessons, and it was with a somewhat strained manner that Miss Drake crossed the room to speak to her at the end of the preparation hour. She had been obliged to find fault with her new pupil several times in the course of the day's classes. There was that in her manner which showed that she feared lest yet another reprimand might be necessary.

"Dreda, have you remembered that to-day is the fifteenth of the month?"

"Yes, Miss Drake."

"Have you the synopsis of the school magazine ready to show me?"

"Yes, Miss Drake."

"Quite ready?"

"Yes, Miss Drake."

The Duck smiled her prettiest, most approving smile.

"Good girl! I like punctuality. Bring it up to me now, please, in my sitting-room."

"Yes, Miss Drake."

Up the stairs ran Dreda, light of foot, bright of eye, heart beating high with happiness, into the bare empty schoolroom, where the windows stood open and the fire smouldered on the grate. She switched on the electric light, crossed the floor to her own desk, and threw open the lid. Stupid! She had imagined that she had left the manuscript book on top ... How came she to be mistaken in so strong an impression?

... She lifted a pile of exercise sheets, pushed the books aside, and scattered miscellaneous possessions to right and to left. Her eyes distended as if about to fall from her head. She sank back on a chair and gazed stupidly before her. The synopsis had disappeared!

Chapter Fourteen.

The synopsis had disappeared! Incredible though it seemed, it was but too true. For the first few minutes Dreda was too much stunned to move from her seat, but presently with a painful effort after self-possession, she arose, and began hastily lifting the contents of the desk, and dropping them one by one on the floor. In this way it seemed impossible to overlook anything, but still no sign of the shining black cover met her sight. She scooped everything together with impatient fingers, pushed them back into the desk, and ran breathlessly into the study.

The girls were amusing themselves in various fashions after the fatigues of "prep.," but one and all looked round with expressions of astonishment at the violent opening of the door which heralded the unexpected appearance of the sub-editor, white-cheeked, and tragic of demeanour.

"What in the world's the matter?"

"The list! The synopsis! It's gone! It was in my desk. Miss Drake sent me for it. She is waiting for me now, and it's *gone*: I can't find it. Has anyone moved it? Does anyone know where it's gone?"

The girls' faces lengthened; there was a moment's tense silence, then everyone spoke at once.

"*Dreda*! How dreadful! Are you *sure*? In your desk? No one would take it out of your desk!"

"Dreda! You are *always* mislaying your things. You have put it somewhere else. *Think*! Remember your keys! You vowed you had put them in your glove drawer, and they were found in the box with your best hat."

"Have you been upstairs to look in your cubicle?"

Dreda stamped with impatience.

"Of course I haven't. My cubicle, indeed! As if I would keep a book there! It was in my desk, I tell you. I left it there last night. I saw it with my own eyes this morning. Oh! don't ask silly questions—don't waste time. She is waiting for me. What am I to do?"

"Come!" cried Susan quickly, and sped upstairs towards the classroom, while Dreda followed hard in her wake, leaving the other girls to discuss the situation round the fire. The universal impression was that Dreda had stowed away the book in some hiding-place, and had promptly forgotten all about it. She was always doing it; never a day arrived but she went about inquiring in melancholy accents if anyone had seen her indiarubber, her penknife, her keys, her gloves. She was always leaving things about, and, upon suddenly discovering their presence, popping them into impromptu hiding-places to save running upstairs—behind a photograph, in an empty flower-pot, beneath a mat or cushion, anywhere and everywhere, as circumstances prompted. Nothing was certain but that nine times out of ten she would forget the whole incident, and would have no better clue to help her in her search after the missing article than that she had put it "somewhere!"

"Poor old Dreda!" said Barbara sympathetically. "Hard lines, when she has worked so hard! The Duck will be down upon her like a ton of bricks. She loathes untidiness. Poor old Dreda—she'll get a rowing instead of praise. It's tragic when you think of that fine cover, and all the beautiful black letters!"

"She's been an awful bore. It will do her good to be taken down a bit."

"Poor Dreda all the same. Things that do you good are so *very* disagreeable. I like her enthusiasm, when it doesn't interfere with me! And she's a real good sort. A bore at times, but a good little meaner."

"It's no use meaning, if you don't perform, where The Duck is concerned. I wouldn't be in her shoes."

Meanwhile Dreda had turned out the contents of her desk for a second time, while Susan stood anxiously looking on. When the last paper had fluttered to the ground, the two girls faced one another in eloquent silence.

"It isn't there," said Susan at last. "There must be some mistake. Think, dear! Are you *quite* sure that you put it here, and nowhere else? What did you do after you finished binding the papers? Where did you go? Think of everything you did."

"But I did nothing!" cried Dreda miserably. "I only dressed and went down to supper. I never took it out of this room at all—I'm certain, positive—as certain as I'm alive!"

"But we could look. It is worth while looking. We must find it!"

But at this very moment the door of Miss Drake's room opened, and a quick voice called out a summons.

"Dreda! I am waiting. Kindly come at once."

The colour ebbed still further from Dreda's cheeks, her eyes grew wide and tragic, she extended her hands towards Susan, as if mutely appealing for help, and felt them clasped with a strong protecting pressure.

"You must go, but I'll search. I'm a good looker, you know. Poor darling! It *is* hard, but I'll help—I *will* help."

Then Etheldreda the Ready threw her arms round her friend's neck and cried brokenly:

"Susan, dear Susan, you are good, and I love you! I was horrid about the editorship... You would have been far better than I. This is my punishment—I have brought it on my own head."

Her voice was so sweet, her eyes so liquid and loving, she drew herself up and marched to her doom with so gallant an air, that her faithful admirer thought instinctively of the martyrs of old. She turned and ran hurriedly upstairs.

Meantime Miss Drake sat looking towards the door with an impatient frown. The frown deepened at sight of Dreda's empty hands, and she tapped on the table with the end of her pencil. Dreda's heart sank still further at the sound which Miss Drake's pupils had learnt to associate with their blackest hours.

"You have kept me waiting for ten minutes, Dreda. Where is your manuscript? I have no time to waste."

"I—I—can't—I can't find it, Miss Drake."

85

Miss Drake leant back in her chair and became in a moment a monument of outraged dignity. Looking at her, it was impossible to believe that one had even ventured on the liberty of calling her by so familiar an epithet as "The Duck." She turned her long neck from side to side, elevated her eyebrows, and cleared her throat in an ominous manner.

"I am afraid I don't understand. You told me a few minutes ago that everything was ready."

"So it was. In my desk. I left it there last night—I went to find it just now, and—it's gone! Disappeared. I can't *think* what has happened. It was bound like a book. It looked beautiful. It's not my fault!"

"Nonsense, Etheldreda!" cried Miss Drake sharply. "If you had put it in your desk, it would be there still. This is just another example of your careless, unmethodical habits. You have put the book in some unlikely, out-of-the-way corner, and have forgotten all about it. I feared some *contretemps* of the kind, and was much relieved when you told me that all was ready. I am very much disappointed and annoyed!"

"Miss Drake, it *was* there! I'm absolutely positive. I never was surer of anything in my life than that I left it there last night, and saw it again this morning."

Miss Drake shrugged her shoulders expressively.

"Extravagant assertions do not prove anything, Etheldreda. In a case of this sort I judge by previous experience. I have repeatedly warned you about your careless habits, but apparently without success. In this case you had a responsibility to fulfil for others as well as yourself, which should have made you doubly careful. You had better continue your search in the other rooms."

"It is no good, Miss Drake. The book *was* in the desk."

Dreda kept her place stolidly, and there was a settled conviction upon her face which Miss Drake was quick to note. She watched the girl in silence for several moments, her brow knitted in thought, then suddenly her expression softened and her voice regained its habitual kindly tone.

"If you put it there, my dear child, it must be there still. Perhaps it is! I know your sketchy fashion of looking. See! I will come and help you to look again. Perhaps we shall find the book hidden away in a corner where you have never thought of looking!"

Dreda thought ruefully of the scattering of her treasures which had twice over left the desk bare and empty, but it seemed easier to allow Miss Drake to see for herself than to protest any further; so she meekly opened the door and followed the governess down the passage. From above could be heard the voices of the girls ascending to dress for the evening; doors opened and shut, and echoes of suppressed laughter floated to the ear. Everybody, Dreda reflected darkly—everybody was happy but herself! She led the way to her desk and opened the lid, revealing the confused mass of books and papers. She was miserably resigned to receiving yet another lecture on untidiness, but The Duck smiled in a forbearing fashion, and said:

"You *have* been making hay of your possessions! No wonder you could not find what you wanted. Now what was this book like? You said that the papers were bound."

"A shiny black cover with a paper label on the back."

Miss Drake lifted up the loose papers with her pretty white hands, laid them daintily on one side, and proceeded to examine the exercise books one by one, while Dreda stood by in hopeless silence. One might search all day and all night, but it was impossible to find what was not there. Her eyes looked listlessly on the map book, the arithmetic book, the French exercise book; even the big untidy note book roused no flicker of animation, though if it chanced to fall open it would reveal caricature drawings of school authorities which must needs draw confusion upon her head. She would never have the heart to draw caricatures again! The thick book with the mottled cover contained the compositions which had won praise and distinction. She had felt so proud of the "Excellent" written in pencilled letters at the end of the final sentences. Never again would she know what it was to be happy and gay! The big drawing-book must have suffered from its fall—for the leaves appeared to be bent and doubled back. Dreda felt the calm indifference of despair, but Miss Drake frowned and made a clicking sound of disapproval.

"My dear! Your drawing-book! You are really incorri—"

She stopped short in the middle of the word, for the moment that the drawing-book was opened her quick eye had caught sight of a shiny black cover behind the crumpled papers. She lifted it rapidly, saw the printed label on the back, and held it out towards her pupil with a mingling of triumph and impatience.

"My dear Dreda! What did I tell you? All this fuss for nothing. You are really too trying. Why didn't you look properly before coming to me?"

Dreda's exclamation of bewilderment was echoed by another, as Susan entered the room on her return from her unsuccessful search upstairs. She added her own quiet testimony to Dreda's excited protestations that the synopsis was not, could not conceivably have been in the desk when she had turned it out ten minutes before, but Miss Drake refused to listen. Her temper was ruffled, she enforced silence with an imperative gesture, bade Dreda follow her to the study, and seated herself at her desk with her most severe and school-mistressy expression.

As for Dreda, she feebly dropped into a chair and sat staring blankly before her, the image of limp dejection. The very stars in their courses seemed conspiring to fight against her, for no ordinary, every-day reason could explain the extraordinary happenings of this afternoon! She was so stunned and bewildered that she forgot to watch the effect of the great synopsis on the Editor-in-chief, and so missed a delightful study in expressions, as The Duck's irritation gave place to smiles and dimpling spasms of amusement. It was only after she had finished the reading (after all the labour of production what a short time it took to read), and had asked a word of explanation, that Dreda seemed suddenly galvanised into fresh life, but as usual with her, when the awakening came, it came with a vengeance. She leapt to her feet, and disregarding the question, launched her thunderbolt with dramatic vehemence.

"Miss Drake, I wish to resign being editor."

"Do you, Etheldreda? Why?"

The voice was so calm, Miss Drake's whole manner so devoid of surprise or chagrin, that Dreda felt as if a douche of cold water had been suddenly poured down her back. No kindly protests, no encouragement, no sympathy. Nothing but that cool, level "*Why*?" She stood gaping and hesitating, for in truth it was hard to answer. To say that she was sick of the whole thing because she had encountered a few initial difficulties and worries seemed mean and poor-spirited, and Dreda could not think so lightly of herself. In the minute of hesitation she had lightly brushed aside difficulties, and felt a swelling of righteous renunciation.

"Because—I want Susan to take it. She would do better than I."

"Have you only just discovered that, Dreda?"

The question was put in a tone which Dreda had never heard before from Miss Drake's lips—a tone so tender, so gentle and conciliatory, that it startled as much as the words themselves. Dreda stared, the colour paling on her cheeks, her hands clenched at the back of her chair. What did it mean? Susan had volunteered her services, and Miss Drake had deliberately rejected them in favour of herself, and now she said, she implied— The girl's lips quivered as she spoke again:

"You *chose* me!"

"Why?" asked Miss Drake once more, in the same gentle voice. "*Why*, Dreda? Think a moment! Does it not occur to you, dear, that I might have chosen you, not because the work needed *you*, but because you needed the work? Your duties called for patience, and perseverance, and method, and punctuality, and neatness, and tact—all qualities which needed development in your case; while in Susan's—"

"You would rather have had Susan! You didn't really want me at all!"

The bitter disappointment in the girl's voice went to the hearer's heart. It was one of the hardest tasks which she had ever had to perform to answer truthfully, and so give another pang to the sensitive young heart. The colour rose on her cheeks and her brows twitched nervously, but she would not allow herself to prevaricate.

"Yes, Dreda, dear. For the sake of the work I should have preferred Susan, but I wanted to help you to get the better of your failings. I wanted it so much that I was prepared to undertake the extra work which your carelessness might involve, for the magazine could not be allowed to suffer. I am afraid it is painful to you, dear, to hear this, but if your vanity is wounded, you can comfort yourself with the remembrance that I was so much interested in you, so anxious for your improvement, that I rejected a most capable helper on your account."

"Thank you!" sighed Dreda faintly. There was not a sign of irritation or resentment in her manner, and her thanks were evidently genuine. She might have posed as an image of humility and abasement as she stood with bowed head and downcast eyes before the desk. The swing of the pendulum had brought her into the valley of humiliation, and in characteristic fashion she felt a melancholy pleasure in playing her part as thoroughly as possible. "Thank you. You are very good. I am very grateful. We have to learn our lessons in life, I suppose, but it's hard at the time. It's been a great *shock*, but it's good for me, I suppose. I can never be careless again. I've read in books about something happening and finishing the girl's youth. I feel like that now! You meant me to learn, and I *have* learnt, so there's no need to go on. You can have Susan, and no more bother—"

Miss Drake's lips twitched in a smile which fortunately Dreda did not see.

"I think not, Dreda. I should prefer to keep to present arrangements. If you have really learnt your lessons so quickly there will be no 'bother' to fear. You may go now, dear. We will discuss the synopsis later on. I dare say you will like to have a little quiet time before dinner. Come to me to-morrow at the same hour."

Dreda backed silently from the room a picture of tragic despair, and slowly mounted to the dormitory where the faithful Susan awaited her coming. The two girls faced one another in silence for several moments before Dreda spoke.

"Susan! on your word of honour will you answer me a question truthfully?"

"Yes, Dreda, of course I will."

"Why did you offer to be sub-editor after I had asked?"

Poor Susan! The freckles disappeared in a crimson blush which mounted to her temples, and tinged her very neck beneath the stiff brown band. She twisted her fingers together, and stammered incoherent nothings.

"Go on! You promised. The truth, and nothing but the truth."

90

"Dreda, dear—"

"Go on! I'm prepared. I've suffered so much humiliation already that a little more or less doesn't matter. Well?"

"I thought—I was afraid—I didn't want you to get into trouble, dear. You are so clever, and original, and sparkling, it is natural that you should get tired. I am just a dull, plodding old machine."

Dreda bent her tall young head and kissed her friend with an air of humble adoration.

"You are good and true, and I wronged you. I thought you were as despicable as myself. All my life long I shall try to be worthy of your forgiveness. My heart's broken, Susan! Everyone despises me in this school, and I've an enemy, a secret enemy, who is hiding like a snake in the grass. You know perfectly well that that book was not in the desk when we looked!"

Susan was silent. She was as sure of the fact as it was possible to be, but her cautious nature reminded her of the possibility of mistake, and she would not venture on a definite assertion.

"I *thought* it was not; I *thought* we turned out everything."

"I *know* we did! It was the work of mine enemy. Some day I'll discover her, and then—"

Susan looked sharply upwards.

"What then?"

"I'll heap coals of fire on her head! I'll forgive her, and try to lead her into better ways. That's all that's left to me now—to be a beacon to others!" Dreda's voice shook, her composure breaking down before the force of her own eloquence. She sank down on her bed, and the tears rolled down her cheeks. "Oh! Oh! My heart will break. If it wasn't for the exeat next week I should lie down and die. I'm going home! They love me there. I never, never valued it before. I'm going home to mother and the girls!"

Chapter Fifteen.

It was a very subdued, a very humble, a touchingly affectionate Etheldreda who made her appearance at The Meads a few days later, and her mother and sisters regarded her demeanour with anxious curiosity.

"Poor darling, poor darling! She is so sweet and quiet—I'm glad, of course; *very* glad," repeated Mrs Saxon, with a forced emphasis, which seemed to show that she needed to convince herself of her own sincerity, "but it seems so short a time to have brought about such a change. I'm afraid she has been unhappy!"

Rowena stared thoughtfully at the fire. Her face looked older, the cheeks less rounded, the red lips dropping at the corner. She was a beautiful girl, but the old sparkle had given place to an air of weary endurance sad to see on a young face. At the moment when she had expected most of life, she had been obliged to give up her dreams, and to accept in their place a monotonous, uneventful existence, which left too much time for the indulgence of her own thoughts. The weather was depressing, visitors few and far between, and, from a girl's point of view, lacking in interest when they did arrive. Maud was stupid and obstinate, Dreda and the boys at school, and the parents depressed. Lessons, walking, and practising occupied the days until four o'clock, then the curtains were drawn, the lamps lit, and each afternoon afresh Rowena counted up the long hours which must elapse before bedtime, and asked herself how she could get through the time. Poor Rowena! She had counted the days until Dreda's return, and now felt yet another pang of depression at meeting this subdued edition of her lively sister. She sighed in melancholy, long-drawn fashion, while Maud wriggled and grimaced.

"I expect she's *misunderstood*. There's lots of people are, besides the book. I know One who is. She's misunderstood by people who think they know best, and are always scolding and finding fault. 'Tis better far to rule by love than fear.' *I* shall, when I'm big. You could do something then, but when people are always grumbling, it's no use trying. I expect Dreda has some one like that, and it's broken her spirit. If you don't let her leave, she'll pine away and die!"

"Is that what you contemplate doing yourself beneath the persecution of the people, or person, to whom you so eloquently refer? I must give you a lesson in nominatives to-morrow, my dear. They are evidently another point which is misunderstood," retorted Rowena with cutting composure. It was one of the little encounters which was daily, almost hourly, taking place between the two sisters, whose widely differing dispositions seemed to jar more than ever in the close relationship of teacher and pupil. Mrs Saxon was greatly troubled by the continual friction, and she, like her daughter, had been anxiously looking forward to Dreda's visit as a healthful enlivening influence which could not fail to do good. And now Dreda was so mysteriously subdued and silent! What had happened to change the child so strangely in six short weeks?

As for Miss Dreda herself, she was not only conscious of, but felt an acute enjoyment in observing the anxiety of her relatives on her behalf, and, like a true actress, warmed to her part under the consciousness of an audience. The more intently did her mother's eyes regard her, the more meek and downcast became her air; she figuratively turned the other cheek to Maud's tactless sallies, and played humble handmaid to Rowena's lightest wish. For one whole day—and then of a sudden weariness fell upon her. She reflected with horror that only two more days of the exeat remained, and determined to waste not another moment in repining. Within five minutes' time from the forming of this decision Maud was dumbfounded to find herself brutally snubbed, while a request from Rowena was received with a callous exhortation to "Do it yourself!"

"I was wondering how long it would last," said Rowena, with a smile. "It was really an admirable impersonation, but what was the idea, Dreda? I can't quite see what you were driving at, but I suppose there was some reason behind!"

"Yes, there was; several reasons! I've recovered, Rowena, because I am young and elastic, and time is a wonderful healer—but I've been through awful difficulties! Treachery and humiliation, and things turning to dust and ashes when you expected to enjoy them most. Talk of martyrdoms!"— Dreda rolled her eyes to the ceiling—"I look back, my dear, to the time when I lived quietly at home, and I can't believe it was the same person!"

"Rubbish! Bunkum! Bosh! What high-falutin' you talk, Dreda! You're not changed a bit, and I'm glad of it, for, oh, my dear, I *have* missed you! I've been *so* dull! Come down from your stilts and talk sensibly. I'm aching for a good old talk."

Dreda beamed with delight. Here was appreciation! No sign of superiority, no condescension from a young lady in long frocks and done-up hair towards a schoolgirl fledgling, but an open avowal of need, an invitation to a heart-to-heart talk on a basis of affectionate equality. She clasped her hands together in the intensity of her delight, and hitched her chair nearer her sister.

"Yes, yes, let's talk, let's—let's *grumble*! We're both in the dumps, and it's so cheering to grumble and get it off your mind. Go on, you're the eldest—you've the first turn. Is it Maud?"

"Oh, Maud! Maud is enough to drive anyone crazy; but she's only a part."

"What's the rest?"

Rowena leant her head on her hand and stared out of the window. The garden was dank and deserted, the country beyond showed no sign of habitation; the wind moaned among the tall, bare trees.

"Dreda," she asked unexpectedly, "am I pretty?"

Dreda's grey eyes widened with surprise.

"What in the world has that to do with it?" she asked curiously. "Pretty? Yes, of course. Awfully, when you're in a good temper. We all are. It's in the family. Do you know what Susan calls us?—the youngest Currant Bun, you know—'The Story-Book Saxons.' Isn't it a jolly name? Because, she says, we look as if things would happen to us like they do to people in a book."

"Well, they don't to me, anyway. That's just it! What's the use of being pretty if one is buried alive? Think of it, Dreda! nothing has happened all these six long weeks, except old ladies coming to call, and going to tea with mother at the vicarage. I should think there never was such a dull place. We didn't notice before, because it was holiday time, and the house was full, but it's awful for a permanency. The nearest interesting girl lives four miles off, the others are too boring for words. I asked one of them if there were ever any dances, and she laughed and asked whom we should dance with. There are only three young men within a radius of miles. There might perhaps be a Hunt Ball at C— next autumn. ... And I thought I should have a London season!"

Dreda meditated, hunched up in her chair, her chin resting upon her hand. For the moment the scarcity of dances did not affect herself, but she loyally endeavoured to regard the situation from her sister's point of view.

"Are the three young men *nice*?"

"Oh, my dear, what does it matter? There aren't enough of them to count. Bob Ainslie is one; he used to come over to umpire for the boys' cricket matches. You remember him—freckles and stick-out ears. He has a moustache now. I expect he's quite nice, but he is *not* exciting. Another is Frank Ross, at the Manor House—I believe he is generally in town. And that nice old Mrs Seton has a son, too. He's handsome; I've seen him riding along the lanes; but, of course, he doesn't pay afternoon calls. What are you to do in a neighbourhood where there are no nice girls, and two and a half young men?"

"Improve your mind!" returned Dreda glibly. "Providence evidently doesn't mean you to move in the social round. Perhaps if you had, you'd have grown proud and worldly. I think myself you *would*, for I saw symptoms of it before we left town. Perhaps you've got to be chastened—" Dreda stopped short with a hasty remembrance that she had promised to sympathise, not exhort, and added hurriedly: "Maud's enough to chasten anyone! It's sickening for you, dear, for you would have had lots of fun, and been the belle wherever you went. Let's pretend the Hunt Ball is to-night, and you are going to make your *début*, a radiant vision in white satin—no, satin's too stiff!—silver tissue. Yes, yes! Silver tissue—how perfectly lovely!—and a parure of matchless diamonds flashing like a river of light upon your snowy neck."

"*Débutantes* don't wear diamonds, and it's not snowy. These boned collar bands leave horrid red marks. An antique medallion of crystal and pearl swung on a silver chain—"

Dreda pranced up and down on her chair in delighted appreciation.

"Yes! Yes! You're splendid, Ro; you know just what to say! And a feather fan, with a tiny mirror let into the sticks; dear little silver shoes with buckles, and a single white rosebud tucked in your hair below your ear. That's the place they always put it in books. It would fall out before the first waltz was over, but no matter! Then your opera cloak. That must be white, too—ermine, I think, or perhaps white fox, worth hundreds and hundreds, that a Russian prince had sent you in token of his devotion. Oh, my dear, my dear; what an *angel* you would look!"

Rowena laughed gaily. Her cheeks had grown pink, and her blue eyes sparkled with enjoyment.

"Dreda, Dreda! What a mad hatter you are! Where *did* you get such ridiculous ideas?"

But it was evident that the ideas, ridiculous though they might be, were by no means unpleasing, and Dreda was about to venture forth on a fresh flight of imagination when, to the annoyance of the sisters, the door opened and Maud, the stolid and unimaginative, stood on the threshold.

"No admittance, Maud. Go away! We're having a private talk."

"I can't go away. It's business. Something awful's happened!" announced Maud calmly. "A man's called, and Mason said mother was in, and she's out, and he's in the drawing-room, and it's rude to send him away. I came to tell you."

"A *man*! What man?"

"The Seton man. The young one with the nose."

The two elder girls exchanged quick, eloquent glances.

"Are you *sure* mother is out? She was in half an hour ago."

"She's out now. She went across the fields to bandage the hand of the baby that the kettle scalded in the white cottage in the dip. You'll have to see him instead."

Rowena turned a face of despairing resignation upon her sister.

"In this blouse! A flannel blouse. Oh, Dreda—the contrast. Think of the silver tissue!"

Dreda looked, and her face was eloquent. Truth to tell, the flannel blouse, though neat and tidy, as were all Rowena's garments, could by no manner

96

of means be called becoming. It did seem tragic to appear to an interesting stranger under such disadvantageous circumstances.

"You must change it!" she cried hastily. "Put on your blue dress; you look ripping in that. I'll go in for a minute, and tell him to stay while I run for mother; by that time you'll be ready, and can talk till she gets back. I'll tell Mason to get tea. Fly! You are so quick, you can be ready in five minutes."

Rowena flew, and Dreda smoothed her hair with her hands and prepared to leave the room in her wake, but Maud's square figure blocked the way, and Maud's voice demanded instantly:

"And what shall *I* do?"

"You? Nothing! It's not your affair. Go up to the nursery and keep quiet."

Maud gurgled with indignation. Not her business, indeed! She who had been first on the scene, and had carried the message! Dreda was hateful! Simply hateful! After pretending to be so good, too. "Nursery, indeed! *I'll* show her!" growled Maud eloquently.

Guy Seton was standing before the fire as the door opened in Etheldreda's impetuous hand, and the man and the girl stared at each other in mutual admiration and approval. "Fair hair, clean shaven, twinkly eyes, big shoulders, Norfolk suit, gaiters. I do *love* men in country clothes," decided Dreda in a mental flash. "Halloa! whom have we here? A schoolgirl daughter. What a pretty, bright-looking girl!" thought the young man almost as quickly. Then they shook hands and Dreda plunged into explanations.

"How do you do? It's so stupid. Mother's out! The maid didn't know, but she has gone across the fields to see a little boy who upset the kettle. Burnt, you know! Mother dresses it. If you will sit down and wait a few minutes, I'll run and bring her back."

Mr Seton smiled, a delightful twinkly smile.

"Oh, please don't hurry her. I should be so sorry. You mustn't trouble about me. I can call another day."

But this was not at all what Dreda desired, and her voice took a tone of keen personal entreaty as she replied:

"Oh, please don't go away! Mother can finish the dressing and be back in ten minutes from now, and I've ordered tea, and my sister will give it to you while you wait. We have so few callers, and it's such a dull, wet day. Do *please* stay and have tea!"

At that the smile gave place to a laugh. Mr Seton found it altogether delightful to be welcomed in so appreciative a fashion, and told himself that it was a treat, indeed, to meet a girl so natural and unaffected. He made no further demur, but when Dreda left the room sat down in a comfortable chair and stretched his long legs towards the fire, smiling to himself with obvious enjoyment of his recollections. It was indeed a grey wintry afternoon, and he was by no means averse to sitting by this cheery fire, looking forward to tea and further conversation with "Miss Golden-locks."

And the sister who was to entertain him meantime—that must be Miss Saxon, the grown-up daughter of whom he had heard, though he did not know her by sight. He did not care for grown-up girls as a rule, they were too self-conscious and self-engrossed—schoolgirls were far more fun. Then the door creaked once more, and he started to his feet to behold a square, stolid form advancing towards him, and to receive a pompous greeting from Maud, who had waited only until Dreda was safely out of the house, and had then hurried into the drawing-room determined to enjoy "her turn" before Rowena arrived.

"How do you do? My mother will soon be here. My sister has gone to fetch her. I hope you are quite well."

"Perfectly so, thank you. I hope you are the same. To whom have I the pleasure of speaking?" inquired Mr Seton, with a sudden change of demeanour which said much for his powers of adaptability. With Dreda he had been all candour and friendliness; confronted with Maud he became at once a solemn model of decorum.

"I am Maud—Maud Saxon. We are all named to match, because we are Saxons by name as well as appearance. You are the Mr Seton who lives in the grey house at Fenley. I have seen you on the roads riding a grey cob with a white nose."

"Very probably. He is a great treasure. Are you interested in horses? Perhaps you ride yourself!"

"I did once, but I don't now. We're *rejuiced*!" announced Maud, rolling out the new word with an enjoyment at which the hearer had much ado to retain his composure. "We used to keep five horses, and ride in the Row, but horses cost too much now. Stables and grooms, and things to eat, and, of course, they may die. We've got nothing now except the car, and that saves money, for you can bring home the stores from the station, and drive Dreda to school, and save the fares."

"Just so," said Mr Seton dryly. "Gars are most useful. Especially in the country." Maud had taken possession of a chair at the opposite side of the fireplace, and as he looked at her square, solemn face, he prayed that it would not be long before Mrs Saxon and her elder daughter returned. "Do you also go to school?"

"No," Maud pursed her lips with an injured air. "Dreda was going to a finishing school in Paris this term, and I had a resident governess. Then— we were 'rejuiced,' and she had to go to a cheaper one at Horsham. That was her *trial*. There are horrid girls there, and she's misunderstood, and when she came home she was so quenched you wouldn't know her, but after a day she was just as bad as ever. And our governess went away, and Rowena teaches me, to save expenses. She hates it, and so do I. She hasn't enough patience for training the young."

Guy Seton privately thought that quite a large stock of patience would be required to train this particular specimen of the young. He was embarrassed by the personal note of Maud's confessions, and cast about in his mind for a means of changing the conversation. The elder sister! Was she in the house? Could she be expected to appear?

"Is Miss Saxon at home? I should like to see her before I go."

Maud nodded solemnly.

"She's coming! She's changing her dress. She had on a flannel blouse, and rushed upstairs to put on her best frock when she heard you were here."

"You little wretch!" cried Guy Seton, mentally. The colour mounted to his face in mingled anger against the offender, and sympathy for the absent sister whose efforts on his behalf had been so ruthlessly betrayed, but before he had time to reply in words a sudden sound from behind attracted his attention, and he turned, to behold the blue-robed figure of Rowena standing in the doorway, her face white and set, her wide reproachful eyes fixed on her sister's face!

Chapter Sixteen.

It was an awkward moment for all three occupants of the room. The young man stood, flushed and silent, looking from one sister to the other, conscious of an increasing anger towards Maud, and a kindly and chivalrous sympathy for the confusion of her sister. Poor girl! She was too young, had too little experience of the world to carry off the situation with a laugh. A young woman of society would have seized the opportunity for cementing a friendship, would have swept gaily forward holding out her skirts, and laughingly demanding his approval, but Rowena could do none of these things, her utmost efforts could succeed only in hiding the signs of confusion beneath a frosty coldness of demeanour.

How unnatural was this manner was plainly demonstrated by the behaviour of the offender herself. At the first moment of Rowena's appearance Maud had appeared embarrassed indeed, but with a fearful joy mingling with her shame, the joy of one who has greatly dared, and is prepared to endure the consequences; but when Rowena swept forward, calm and stately, when she seated herself and began to talk polite nothings, with never so much as a word or a glance in her own direction, then, visibly and unmistakably, terror fell upon Maud's childish heart—she made a bee-line for the door, and slunk hastily out of sight.

"Little wretch!" soliloquised Guy Seton once more. "Lands me into this pleasant position, and then sneaks away, and leaves me to fight it out alone! Poor little girl!"—this last epithet obviously did *not* refer to Maud! "Hard lines to arrive at such an awkward moment. Furious, of course, with the whole three—the child for speaking, with me for hearing, with herself for having given the opportunity! Such a pretty frock, too; and she is ripping in it! Jolly good of her to have taken the trouble, but now I suppose she'll hate the sight of me, and bear me a lasting grudge. Hope to goodness Golden-locks is not long in coming back!"

"Quite a chilly wind. We are so very exposed and open in this house!" Rowena was saying in high, artificial tones. She hailed the arrival of tea with evident relief, and the conversation flowed on a trifle more easily when there was something definite to do; nevertheless both heaved sighs of joy as the sound of Dreda's high, cheery voice was heard from without, and she entered the room by her mother's side.

Guy Seton privately expected Rowena to follow Maud's example and quietly disappear, so he admired all the more the pretty little air of dignity with which she stuck to her post and forced herself to take her natural part in the conversation.

"Plucky little girl! Stands to her guns, and won't allow herself to run away," he told himself approvingly, as he proceeded to unfold the object of his visit.

"We are arranging a small frolic for Friday in the shape of a paper-chase. Everybody within five miles is coming on horseback or bicycles, as suits them best, and we ought to have a good run. We start at eleven prompt from our gates, and return for a scramble luncheon at about two. I hope you will all come!"

His glance wandered from Dreda to Rowena—the first he felt sure would accept with enthusiasm; the latter he feared would politely refuse; but Rowena smiled again, her set meaningless little smile, and allowed a subdued murmur of thanks to mingle with Dreda's rhapsodies. It was cleverly done, for without being in any way committed she had escaped drawing attention upon herself by a refusal; nevertheless as he met her eye, and held her limp, unresponsive hand in his at parting, Guy Seton felt more convinced than ever that whoever else might honour his paper chase, Miss Rowena Saxon would not be among the number!

He walked down the drive twirling his stick in a threatening manner, his face grim and set. It was bad luck indeed to make such a bad beginning with one of the prettiest and most attractive-looking girls he had ever met, and a near neighbour into the bargain. He had a momentary vision of Rowena spinning along on a bicycle, her fair face flushed with exercise, her sweet eyes alight with interest and excitement; and of a sudden it seemed a dull, senseless thing to fly over the country-side, with ordinary everyday neighbours and friends. How ordinary and everyday they seemed, when contrasted with Rowena's stately young grace! And now she was prejudiced against him for ever, and at this very moment was probably denouncing her sister's stupidity, and vowing never willingly to meet him again!

Rowena, however, was doing nothing of the kind. Calm and composed, she sat on beside her mother and Dreda, and declared that the idea of a paper-chase failed to attract her, and that she had no intention of tiring herself out, and running needless risks by riding breathlessly across country on so stupid and frivolous an aim! Mrs Saxon was both puzzled and disappointed, while Dreda expostulated in her usual violent fashion.

"Rowena, how mad! How idiotic! What are you raving about! What's the use of grumbling and growling because there's nothing to do, and no one to see you, and then the moment anyone appears—such a dear, too, with such sweet, twinkly eyes!—to behave like a cold-blooded frog, mincing your words, and looking as if you were made of ice, and then saying you won't go, when it's a chance of no end of fun, and seeing everyone there is to be seen! Idiotic!"

"Dreda! Dreda, dear, really is it necessary to be quite so violent?" Mrs Saxon shook her head in smiling reproach, and Rowena tilted her chin in air, but Dreda refused to be suppressed.

"Oh, mum, dear, *let* me speak as I like! We have to be so proper at school. You can't say a word of slang while the govs. are about, and ordinary language is so *tame*. You can't make a really good effect with ordinary words. Suppose I said to Rowena: 'Your conduct, my dear, is inconsistent, with your sentiments as expressed in conversation,' she wouldn't mind a bit, but when I call her a frog she's furious. Look how she's wagging her head! You can always tell by that when she's in a bait."

"Really, Dreda!" cried Rowena in her turn. She rose from her seat, and sailed haughtily out of the room, disdaining to bandy words with so outspoken a combatant. In truth, she herself was bitterly disappointed in being forced—as she thought—to refuse Mr Seton's invitation, the possibilities of which appealed to her even more strongly than to her sister. To meet a party of young people, to wheel gaily along in the brisk, keen air, laughing and jesting as in the old happy days; to return tired and hungry to the hospitable scramble luncheon—to sit around the fire rested and refreshed, feeling as if those few hours of intimate association had been more successful in cementing friendships than many months of ordinary association. Oh, how tempting *it* sounded! What a blessed change from the level monotony of the last few months! And she needs must give it up, and stay quietly at home, darning stockings, or writing orders to the "Stores," because Maud's blundering tongue has laid her dignity so low, that everything else must needs be sacrificed to its preservation! *Rowena is putting on her best dress—she had on a flannel blouse, and she ran to change it because you were here!* One would need to be nineteen once more to realise the shame, the horror, the distress with which poor Rowena recalled those thoughtless words! She pressed her hands against her cheeks, and gave a little groan of distress. It was characteristic of her that the one thing she now asked was that no one else should know of her humiliation; her mother might remonstrate, and Dreda declaim to her heart's content, but nothing on earth should induce her to disclose the real reason of her refusal. As for Maud, having done the mischief, she might be trusted to keep quiet for her own sake; and even with her, Rowena would have kept silence if she had been allowed. Beyond an added touch of dignity, there was no change in her manner towards her younger sister, but, strange to say, the culprit was by no means satisfied to escape so easily. Maud suffered from an insatiable desire to be observed, and—so to speak—live in the public eye. If she could be observed with admiration, so much the better, but given a choice between being disgraced or ignored, she would not have hesitated for the fraction of a moment. Better a hundred times to be scolded and denounced than to be passed by in silence as if one were a stick or a stone. So it happened that when Rowena treated her with stately indifference, Maud found it impossible to keep silent.

"You might as well say it out!" she declared, wriggling about in her seat, and pouting her lips with an air of offence. "I hate people who bottle things up when all the time you see them fizzling inside. I suppose you're furious with me about what I said."

Rowena drooped her eyelids, and smiled a smile of haughty detachment.

"It is a matter of perfect indifference to me *what* you say."

"It was quite true!"

"Perfectly true. I should be the last person in the world to accuse you of imagination."

"You *were* furious. You went white with rage, and he saw it as well as me. Now, I suppose you'll tell mother, and stop me going to the chase."

"I should not dream of interfering with your plans. It is a matter of perfect indifference to me whether you go or stay."

"But,"—Maud's eyes positively bulged with excitement—"I might say something else. You never know."

"Possibly you might. What then? Do you really imagine, my dear Maud, that anyone notices what *you* say!"

Maud wriggled and spluttered, trying in vain to think of something scathing to say in return. Compared with this lofty indifference the most violent denunciations would have been enjoyable. "Nobody noticed what she said!" Rowena could not have launched an arrow which would have rankled more bitterly. For the remaining hours of that day Maud crept about with a melancholy hang-dog expression, taking little or no part in the general conversation.

The next morning Rowena held firmly to her decision, and the two younger girls were obliged to start without her, Maud unfeignedly relieved, Dreda irritated and perplexed. Something must have happened to account for so unreasonable a change of front, something that had been said or done during that quarter of an hour during which she herself had been absent from the drawing-room. So much was certain, but what could it be? Rowena refused to be questioned, and Dreda was all unsuspicious of the fact that Maud had ventured to interview the visitor on her own account, and so had no suspicions in her direction. The first doubt arose when Guy Seton shook hands with both sisters as with old friends; this fact, combined with Maud's blushing discomfiture, gave Dreda a flash of insight, but for the moment she was more occupied with the young man's very evident disappointment at Rowena's absence.

"Is Miss Saxon not coming?"

"No. I'm so sorry. She sent apologies."

"Is she quite well?"

"Oh, yes, thanks." Dreda was too honest to plead the conventional headache. "She said two were enough. She is going to bicycle to Smitton this morning for some stupid messages. I did my best to make her come."

"I'm sure you did," said the young man kindly. Dreda, looking at him, saw him murmur "Smitton" below his breath, and knit his brows in thought. A minute later he walked away to speak a few farewell words to the hares, who were mounted on horseback, bearing fat bags of paper fragments on their saddles, after which he returned with a smiling face to keep Dreda entertained until "The Meet" had begun to assemble. Excitement and anxiety not to be late had caused the sisters to arrive before their time, but Dreda could not regret the fact, for it was so interesting to watch the new arrivals on horseback and bicycles; to greet old acquaintances, be introduced to new, and finally to meet a beam of welcome from Susan's brown eyes as the Currant Buns wheeled up in a line. Even the sober Mary had condescended to join the chase.

"Fresh air is a tonic. With so much mental exercise on hand I considered it would be a saving of time to spend a day in the open," she said confidentially to Dreda, as she polished her glasses on a large pocket-handkerchief, and replaced them over the red rim on her nose. Dreda sidled carefully away from her side, and when the moment came for the start, was delighted to find Guy Seton riding determinedly by her side.

"I thought you would be on horseback," she said, then looking at him with faintly curious eyes: "Why aren't you, when you have a horse all ready? It's so *much* more interesting than bicycling."

"Sometimes," said Guy, smiling. He waited a moment or two, and then added tentatively: "If you are fond of riding, and would accept a mount sometimes, I'd be delighted to give you one. Our horses have not half enough exercise. I've a nice quiet mare—"

"Oh, thanks, but give me spirit! None of your quiet mares for me. But I am at school; there's no chance for a free day for another three months. This is only the exeat; we go back to-morrow, worse luck!"

"To-morrow! That's very soon. I'm glad I arranged the chase for to-day. You are at Horsham, aren't you?"

Dreda turned her head quickly.

"Yes! Who told you?"

"Your sister. The young one—the one who is here to-day."

"Oh, Maud! Did she come into the drawing-room with Rowena yesterday?"

"Before then. She amused me after you left until Miss Saxon arrived."

"Oh–h!" Dreda's face clouded uneasily. How had Maud amused him? What had she said? In what fashion had she managed to prejudice Rowena against so amiable and kindly a neighbour, for she had now not a moment's doubt that Maud was the cause of the trouble. She determined to put a few leading questions.

"What else did she tell you? She's a dreadful child. We never know what she is going to say next. I don't believe she knows herself. What did she say?"

"Oh, nothing particular! G–general information—don't you know—general information," stammered Guy Seton uncomfortably. But Dreda was not to be put off the scent. She stared at him fixedly, noted his rising colour, and nodded in quiet conviction.

"I know! I can guess one thing at least. She told you we were *rejuiced*."

"I—I—" he began to stammer again, but the corners of his mouth twitched, and the next moment they were laughing together in hearty, youthful enjoyment.

"Too bad of you! Why are you so abnormally sharp? Have pity on my embarrassment," he pleaded, while Dreda shook her yellow mane in derision.

"You are not embarrassed a bit! You laughed before I did! It's easy to guess, because that's Maud's favourite subject at present. She overheard the servants talking, and took a fancy to the word, and now she drags it in on every possible occasion. What else did she say? Anything about me?"

"Er—er—"

"She did! I know she did. Don't try to deny it. Was it—nice?"

"Er—" stammered Guy Seton once more, whereupon Dreda drew herself up with sudden dignity.

"You shouldn't have *allowed* it! She is only a child; you should not have allowed her to talk personalities—"

"But I tried to stop her—I did, indeed! I was most uncomfortable. I tried to change the conversation, but it was no good. Please don't scold me, I've suffered enough as it is!"

"*How* have you suffered?" Dreda's eyes widened eagerly. Now she was on the track of the mystery, and determined to push her inquiries until all was made plain. "*Who* made you suffer?"

"Miss Sax—," said Guy involuntarily, and then quickly drew himself up. "I mean—it's rather awkward for a fellow, don't you know, to listen to things that he ought not to hear—that are not his business—that would annoy other people if they happened to overhear."

He flushed as he spoke, and Dreda beamed at him with undisguised approval. He was so boyish and honest, so blunderingly transparent, that she felt quite elderly in comparison—a very Sherlock Holmes of diplomacy!

"And what was it that Rowena *did* overhear? Oh, I guessed there was something! She would never have refused to come to-day unless something had happened to offend her. She has such a dull time of it, poor dear, and she loves a change. What did Maud say?"

"Miss Dreda, if your sister didn't tell you herself, do you think I ought to repeat a thing that has already annoyed her?"

"Certainly you ought. It's my business to know, so that I can make things right. I could easily explain—"

Guy gave a short, irritated laugh.

"There's nothing to explain! Your young sister made an indiscreet remark which Miss Saxon overheard as she came into the room. It is only human nature, I suppose, to vent her annoyance upon me, but it's hard luck all the same, for I could not help myself, and it was horribly embarrassing for me too!"

"But *what* did she say?"

Then with another twitch of the lips Guy repeated Maud's betrayal, at which Dreda was at once horrified and amused.

"The little wretch! I shouldn't have minded a bit myself, but when you are grown up it's different! Poor old Ro! It was my fault, for I made her do it. I wanted you to see her in that jolly blue."

"Thanks, so much! It was worth seeing; but it's a pretty big price to pay if your sister is prejudiced against me for life. Perhaps you had better not refer to the subject directly. If I read her aright the less that is said about it the better she will be pleased; but if you get a chance you might speak a good word for me sometimes. I'm not such a conceited fool as to imagine that she took any more trouble for me than she would have done for any other caller who happened to come along, and I've a wretched sort of memory. If I choose to forget a thing, it's surprising how easily I can do it. It would be so jolly if she could manage to forget it too, and start afresh."

"Leave it to me!" cried Dreda, with the air of a young oracle. She had not the slightest idea what she was about to do, but, as ever, had not the slightest doubt of success in tackling a difficult situation. For the moment, however, she felt that she had devoted enough attention to Rowena's affairs, for the excitement of the paper-chase increased with every mile as the track was discovered, only to be lost again and again, forcing the cavalcade to wheel about in all directions searching for the little snow-like flakes of paper which were again to guide them forward.

When a couple of hours had passed Dreda was quite oblivious that the circling paths had led the chase to the little village of Smitton, and was therefore overcome with surprise to come face to face with no less a person than Rowena herself at the corner of the high road. Rowena would have passed by with a bow, but she was instantly surrounded by a little party of friends, all eager to greet her, and to inquire why she had not joined the chase. Guy Seton dismounted with the rest, and stood silently in the background until the first rush of inquiries were over, when, meeting Rowena's eye, he made a simple straightforward request.

"As you have finished your messages, Miss Saxon, won't you join us for the rest of the morning? We could send a wire from the post office if you think Mrs Saxon would be anxious. Please say yes!"

There was nothing extravagant about the manner of his invitation, perhaps in courtesy he could hardly have said less, but there was a transparent sincerity about those last three words which it was impossible to ignore.

Rowena hesitated. Poor Rowena! What a morning of heartache and disappointment it had been. Ten minutes ago, five minutes ago, she had been wheeling along her solitary way, all melancholy and dejection, and behold, one turn of the road and she was in the midst of a merry cavalcade, and the chance which she had thrown away was once more within her grasp.

She hesitated, and half a dozen voices answered in her stead. Of course, she must come! Of course! After this fortunate meeting she could not be allowed to escape. She could not be so cruel as to refuse, and then once again Guy Seton's voice repeated those three quiet words: "Please say yes!"

Well, she was only longing to accept, and having been duly entreated, gave way with a blush and a smile which made her look as pretty as a picture. The cavalcade carried her off in triumph, and Guy Seton kept discreetly in the background, waiting until time should give him his opportunity. His acquaintance with this charming girl had had an unfortunate beginning; he was determined that no haste or imprudence on his own part should give it a second check, but that afternoon Master Leonard Merrick, the hare, went home, made happy by a tip the amount of which was truly princely in his schoolboy estimation!

Chapter Seventeen.

Six months had passed by. The elder pupils at Horsham had gone tremblingly through the ordeal of the Oxford senior examination in July, and Mary, having achieved distinction in three separate subjects, was now busy preparing for the mathematical group of the Cambridge higher local examination in December. She was eventually going on to college, and intended to devote her life to teaching, to which prospect she looked forward with an equanimity which Dreda regarded with mystified amazement.

"And you *like* it! You are content to think of spending your life in a schoolroom, going over and over the same dull old books, Mary! How *can* you?"

But Mary could very easily, it appeared.

"Why not, Dreda?" she inquired. "The books are not dull to me, and surely it is a noble and interesting life to hand on the lamp of learning from one generation to another. It's the work that appeals most to me. Ever since I was a child I have wished to be a schoolmistress."

"Oh, well, I shouldn't mind it myself—for a time," Dreda conceded carelessly. "When one has suffered under the yoke, *it* would be a kind of satisfaction to boss it oneself for a change. I'd quite like to be a headmistress—a horribly strict Head—and make all the girls c–c–ringe before me—for a term, say; but after that—no thank you! I want a wider scope for my life than a stupid old school-house."

Mary smiled, in an elderly, forbearing fashion.

"We are all different, dear Dreda. It would not do if we were made alike. You and I have not the same vocation."

"No; I shall marry," announced Dreda, blandly unconscious of the inference of her words. "I am one of the old-fashioned womanly girls—(it says in the papers, 'Would there were more of them!')—who shine best in their own homes. I'm not learned, and I don't pretend to be; but I can keep house, and order servants about, as well as anybody, and I intend to be very hospitable and give lots of dinners and parties and make my husband proud of me by being the best-dressed woman in the room, and so witty

111

and charming that everything will go with a roar. That's all I want. I haven't an ambitious nature."

Mary's long upper lip looked longer than ever as she listened to this egotistical tirade. She was a plain-looking girl, and the lack of humour in her composition made her somewhat dull and unattractive in manner; but she possessed great strength of character, and was never found lacking in the courage of her opinions. Her opinion at this moment was that Etheldreda Saxon needed a downright good snubbing, and she set herself to administer it without a qualm.

"My dear Dreda, there is nothing in the world you understand as little as your own character. I never met a girl who was so blind to her own defects. Not ambitious! How can you say such a thing in the same breath as that in which you express your longing for admiration? One may be ambitious for unworthy aims as well as for worthy ones; and your desires are all for poor, worldly things which pass away, leaving no one better or wiser. It is false modesty to say you are not clever; you would not allow anyone else to make such a statement unchallenged. If you chose to exert yourself to overcome your faults of carelessness and frivolity, you might take a very fair average position among your companions."

To say that Dreda was taken aback by this very candid criticism of her character is to state the matter far too calmly. She turned white with agitation, and the pupils of her eyes dilated until they appeared to cover the entire iris. It was characteristic of her that it was not anger which so affected her, but real honest horror and distress that a fellow-creature should live and entertain so poor an opinion of her delightful self. She was not, it was true, particularly devoted to Mary, but it had never for a fraction of a second occurred to her that Mary could be otherwise than enthusiastically loyal to herself. And now that the horrible truth was disclosed, her absorbing desire was to reform so mistaken an attitude of mind as speedily as possible.

"Oh, Mary!" she cried tragically. "How you misjudge me! How little you know my real inmost nature! Ask mother—ask Rowena—ask anyone who knows me well; they will all tell you the same thing—I am all heart. I live on my affections; I don't want anything but just to be happy, and have people love me. What have I ever said or done to you that you should think such perfectly horrid things? It hurts me to be misjudged—it hurts awfully! It's like a knife sticking into my heart."

"Because you want to be praised, and can't endure reproof, even if it is for your good. It isn't *pleasant* to find fault, Dreda," declared Mary judicially; "but if I don't speak out I may blame myself in the future. I am afraid of what may happen if you float along as you are doing, blind to your own failings. Some day something may happen to put you to the test, and then you will *fail*, and be humiliated in your own eyes and those of the world."

Dreda regarded her with eyes full of a solemn reproach.

"May you be forgiven, Mary! I forgive you. I'm sorry for your want of charity and understanding. I'm not surprised that you don't understand me; we are made on such different lines; but you ought not to judge.—I don't judge *you*. I think you are very painstaking and industrious. I bear you no ill-will, Mary. I'm only sorry for you."

So far from being melted by this touching forgiveness, Mary flushed with anger, shrugged her shoulders impatiently, and turned back to her desk, whereon lay the first lines of an essay on one of Addison's "Spectator" Essays. An extract from the essay had been given as subject, with the significant words: "Discuss this," inscribed beneath, and Mary's mood was not improved by the fact that with regard to ethical sentiments she seemed to have no idea to discuss. She was fifty times more at home with cut-and-dried figures about the correctness of which there could be no two opinions, whereas Etheldreda the Ready was invariably in the front rank for compositions. The two girls were indeed made "on different lines," and at that moment Mary was not unnaturally provoked to be confronted by a task in which Dreda was undoubtedly her superior.

Dreda was laboriously amiable to her opponent for some days after this "heart to heart" talk, but the endeavour to pour coals of fire was so obvious as to be more irritating than soothing, and Mary had no wish to reopen the discussion. "I've warned her—she must go her own way now. *My* conscience is clear," she told herself stoically, and Dreda went her own way—danced gaily along it, so to speak, and had no thought of danger. She had become accustomed to school routine by this time, and, like most girls, found interest and enjoyment in the full busy life and in the companionship of her kind. She was a favourite with both teachers and scholars, and Susan's quiet devotion could always be counted upon in those moments of need which seemed to be inevitable occurrences in her life. Dreda forgot, and Susan reminded; Dreda procrastinated, and Susan hastened to the rescue; Dreda grew discouraged and Susan cheered; Dreda failed, and Susan succoured; yet with such diffidence were these services performed that self-love felt never a wound, and Dreda was left with the agreeable sense of having conferred, rather than accepted, favours.

"You turn yourself into a nigger slave for Dreda Saxon," grumbled Norah of the spectacles one day when she and Susan walked together in the "crocodile" along a dull country lane. "A regular black, cringing slave—and what thanks do you get for it, I'd like to know? None! Not one little scrap. She's such a bat of self-conceit that she doesn't even know that she *is* helped. If you did a hundredth part as much for other people they'd go off their heads for joy!"

The spectacled eyes rolled wistfully Susan-wards as the last words were spoken, for Norah cherished a schoolgirl's sentimental devotion for her companion, and could not overcome her chagrin at being so completely eclipsed by a new girl—a girl, moreover, who had given to her the undignified nickname of "Gig-lamps," which had been instantly adopted by the whole school. She gazed at Susan as humbly as a dog begging a favour from its master's hand, but no favour was vouchsafed.

"I don't want Dreda to be grateful. I need no thanks. I love her so much that it is my greatest pleasure to be able to help her," said little Susan proudly; but when Norah persistently demanded to know why she had no answer to give. In truth, she herself was sometimes puzzled to account for her own devotion to the hasty, undisciplined creature who fell so far short of her ideal feminine character. Susan's quiet brown eyes were not blinded; probably no girl in the school was more conscious of Dreda's faults, yet her love lived on unchecked by the discovery. She did not realise that it was Dreda's personal beauty and charm which had captivated her imagination, and that all the starved instincts of her beauty-loving nature were finding vicarious satisfaction in another's life. Susan had lived her life in a prosaic household, where beauty was the last consideration to be taken into account. If an article had to be bought, Mrs Webster gave consideration to strength and durability, and to strength and durability alone. In buying curtains, for instance, she sought for a nondescript colour which would defy the sun's rays, a material that would stand repeated washings, and a pattern which would conceal possible stains. A discovery that the cloth would ultimately cut up into desirable dusters was sufficient to give the casting vote of decision, and thereafter draperies of dingy cinnamon would be hung against walls of yellow ochre, with complacent and lasting satisfaction. Amid such drab surroundings Susan had spent her life, and when she looked in the glass it was to see a replica of her sister's faulty features and pallid skin, yet hidden away within that insignificant exterior there burnt the true artist's passion for beauty, for colour, for grace, of which three qualities Etheldreda Saxon was so charming an embodiment. When Susan mentally worked out her novels of the future her heroines invariably wore Dreda's guise, the romantic figures of history took upon themselves Dreda's form, and smiled upon her with Dreda's confident eyes.

The ordinary sentimental school friendship was glorified into a selfless devotion in which her highest joy was found in denying herself for Dreda's good. The two girls—one tall, golden-haired, with vivid colouring and an air of confident strength; the other small, plain, neutral-tinted, timid of mien— were inseparable in work and at play.

Six months' experience of school life had destroyed Dreda's early ardour with regard to examinations. Arithmetic was such a hopeless stumbling-block in her path that it was doubtful whether she would be able to secure a bare pass, and having once realised the fact she readjusted her ambitions with facile speed, announced that she disapproved of modern methods, had no wish to enter the public arena, and was anxious to abandon a course of dangerous cram. Her favourite subject was composition, and here and here alone, she and Susan ran an even race, it being a moot point each week which would gain the highest marks. Susan's essays were more thoughtful, and were written with an apt and dainty choice of words which was a delight to Miss Drake's literary taste, but a certain primness and conventionality still remained to be conquered, in contrast to which Dreda's dashing breeziness of style was a real refreshment. After reading through a dozen essays, all of which began in almost exactly the same words, and ended abruptly after dragging through a dozen commonplace sentences, the tired reader rejoiced at the sight of Dreda's bold handwriting, and was disposed to forgive many failings in gratitude for the one great gift of originality.

Miss Drake was aware of the literary ambitions cherished by the two friends, and in leisure moments sent many a thought into the future, wondering what the years would bring, and if the time would ever arrive when she should say proudly of a well-known writer: "She was my pupil. I helped her towards the goal!" It seemed impossible to prophesy to which of the two girls success would come—Susan of the eloquent brain, the tender heart, or Dreda, with her gift of charm to gild the slightest matter. The young teacher pondered over the question, and one day in so doing there came to her mind a suggestion which promised interest to herself and a useful incentive to her pupils.

The third number of the school magazine would soon be due, and Miss Drake was fully aware of the fact that the sub-editor had grown to regard her responsibilities as a distasteful burden; while the contributors one and all exhibited a lamentable falling away from their early ambitions. Fragments of conversation had reached her ears as she made her way along the corridors. "You must write something—you *must*! I haven't a thing ready."

"You and your old magazine! What a nuisance you are! I've something better to do."

"Here comes Dreda Saxon! Let's hide! She's on the rampage about the mag."

Miss Drake's heart softened towards her "sub" in this difficult plight; she waited a few days to mature her plans, and then made an interesting announcement to the pupils at the conclusion of a history class.

"Before you go, girls, I want to speak to you for a few minutes on another subject. The third number of the school magazine is nearly due, and I am afraid from what I hear that contributions are coming in slowly. You will remember the one condition on which you were allowed to start the paper was that it should be continued for at least two years. One of the lessons you have to learn in life is that a duty once undertaken cannot be lightly thrown aside because it weighs more heavily after the first enthusiasm is past. Steady, quiet perseverance is a great force, and can overcome mountains of difficulty, but,"—she glanced whimsically at the row of depressed young faces—"I am quite aware that it is not a quality which makes a strong appeal at your age, so I propose to be generous, and offer an extra stimulus. You all know the name of Henry Rawdon, one of the greatest—many people think the greatest—writer of our times. He happens to be not only a family connection but my very good friend, and he has promised to help me to carry out a little scheme for your benefit. Instead of the usual nondescript contributions, you will all be required to write an essay on a given subject for the next number of the magazine, and after it has been circulated in the school, the typed papers will be sent to Mr Rawdon, marked with numbers instead of names, and he will judge them, and select the best as the prize number. Miss Bretherton is giving the prize. She is most interested in the competition, and it will be a prize worth having—a complete edition of Mr Rawdon's works, which he has promised to present in person at our breaking-up gathering. Now is that not a splendid stimulus? I hope you feel inspired to do your best to rise to the occasion, and do honour to yourselves and the school." She paused, and the girls stared at her in a solid phalanx of amazement. Henry Rawdon's name was a household word; his works adorned every library worthy the name; it was, in the literal sense of the word, *stunning* to think that such a celebrity should condescend to read their poor little efforts! Etheldreda Saxon was naturally the first to recover her voice.

"And the subject, Miss Drake—what is to be the subject?"

Miss Drake smiled quietly.

"The subject is a very big one, and one on which the youngest girl is as competent to write as the oldest. No one can plead ignorance on this point, or if she does no outsider can give her enlightenment. The subject, chosen by Mr Rawdon himself, is 'My Life—and how I mean to use it.'"

A subdued murmur sounded in the room, the chief notes of which were wonder and dismay. The girls looked at each other with startled looks, their lips fell apart, a blank, half-stupefied expression settled on their faces, as though they found themselves confronted by a task with which they had no power to grapple. But Susan's brown eyes shone like stars; she clasped her little hands tightly together beneath her desk.

Chapter Eighteen.

For the next few days conversation circled incessantly round the subject of the forthcoming literary competition, concerning which there were naturally many diverging opinions. "My life, indeed! *Well*, my first principle has always been 'One thing at a time, and that done well.' I'm cramming for an exam., and have no time to waste on meanderings," declared Barbara, whose compositions invariably received the lowest marks in her form, while Nancy smiled her enigmatical smile, and stared mysteriously into space.

"I shall write it, of course, but I shall not put in my *real* sentiments. It would not be fair to my future. If my plans are to succeed they demand secrecy—breathless, inviolate secrecy, until the hour arrives!"

"Gracious, Nancy! You talk as if you were an Anarchist in disguise!" gasped a horrified voice from the far corner of the fireside round which the girls were assembled, whereupon the gratified Nancy endeavoured to look more mysterious than ever.

"Why in disguise? Is there anything in my appearance which is out of keeping with a life of noble rebellion against tyranny and oppression? A bomb may be often a blessing in disguise, but there is so much narrow prejudice and ignorance in this world that people must be trained to appreciate the true meaning. Till that hour arrives my life's ambition must remain locked within my own breast!"

"I haven't got one—at least, only to have a good time and be done with work. You couldn't put *that* in an essay. It sounds so mean," confessed blue-eyed Flora with a sigh. Dreda looked at her quickly, and as quickly averted her eyes. Put in bald language was not that her own ambition also? In thinking over the essay, she had mentally rehearsed many grandiose phrases; but now, with a sudden chilling of the blood, she realised the emptiness of the high-sounding words. What had she ever wished from life but pleasure, approbation, and easy success? How much thought had she given to possible trials and difficulties? How much effort to train herself for the battle of life? It was one of those blinding moments of self-revelation which come to us all, and before which the noblest natures shrink aghast. Dreda leant her head against the wall to hide herself from the dancing firelight, but her unusual silence could not fail to attract attention, and Norah was quick with a gibing question.

"Why so silent, Etheldreda the Ready? Can it be that you have been so busy arranging the lives of other people that you have not had time to think of your own?"

The dart struck home once more, but before there was time to answer Susan rushed to the defence.

"It's just because Dreda *is* thinking that she does not talk. Dreda will win the prize. No one has a chance against her, but it is such a thrilling subject that it will be interesting to try. The difficulty will be to keep within the limit; only three thousand words—"

"Only! My dear, do you know what three thousand words mean? I counted up one sheet of foolscap, and it came to two hundred and fifty. How on earth could one find enough to say about life to fill twelve whole pages?"

Flora was transparently in earnest, her blue, opaque-looking eyes roving from face to face, inviting sympathy and understanding; but Susan gave a clear little laugh of derision.

"I could fill volumes! It's a wonderful, wonderful theme—a voyage into the dark—a battle to be fought, a victory to be won, a mountain to be climbed, or perhaps no mountain at all, but just a long, long road, on a dead level plain. Work and effort, and failure and success, sorrow and joy, and at the end the secret—the great secret—solved at last!"

Susan's voice trembled, her slight little form shook with emotion, she pressed her hands against her knees to still their trembling. The girls stared at the floor, or exchanged furtive glances of embarrassment. Susan was "too too for words" in her high falutin' moods; she talked just like people in books; silly nonsense that no one could understand! She was going to leave school when she was eighteen and help her mother in the house, because the two elder girls wanted to be teachers. Why couldn't she say so straight out, instead of mooning about secrets, and battles, and mountains to be climbed? Flora sniggered into her handkerchief, Barbara gaped, Nancy tilted her head, and rolled her eyes to the ceiling, Dreda wakened out of her dream, and sat up flushed and eager.

"Susan, *stop*! You mustn't! If you tell us your ideas we may copy them without meaning to do it... If you put thoughts into our heads they stay there and grow, and we can't send them away, but they are *yours*. You ought to keep them to yourself."

"My dear, she says she has enough to fill a volume. She needn't grudge a few to her starving friends," cried Nancy in would-be reproach. "Confide in me, Susan dear! I'll sit at your feet, and gobble up all the pearls that you drop, and perhaps in the end I may win the prize myself. I don't see why it should be taken for granted that only two girls have a chance. There's a lot of vulgar prejudice in this school, but Mr Rawdon will judge with an unbiased mind. I have thought more than once when I've been reading his books that the style was rather like my own, and I've a sort of a—kind of a—what's the word?—*premonition* that he'll like me best."

There was a general laugh, but Nancy was a favourite despite her teasing ways, so the laughter was good-tempered and sympathetic, and it was easy to see that if by chance the prize fell to her lot the award would be a popular one. Nancy was incurably lazy, but the conviction lingered in the minds of her companions that "she could be clever if she chose," and it would seem quite in character that she should suddenly wake up to the surprise and confusion of her competitors. Dreda looked round with an anxious air, as if recognising a new, and formidable competitor. She determined to begin making notes that very evening, and asked suddenly:

"Has anyone seen my stylo? My things seem to be bewitched nowadays. They are always disappearing. I searched for my French book for a solid hour yesterday, and this morning it was my penknife, and now it's the pen—I waste half my time hunting and searching."

"You are so untidy. If you would be more methodical—"

"I didn't ask for moral reflections, Barbara. I asked for my pen."

"Is it a black one? A little stumpy black one—about so long?"

"Yes—yes! That's it. Have you seen it, Nancy?"

Nancy stroked her chin with a meditative air.

"I *did* see a stylo somewhere! I remember noticing it—a very nice one. Quite new."

120

"Yes—yes; that's it. Where was it? Do think, Nancy! Cudgel your brains."

"I am cudgelling them—I'm cudgelling *hard*." Nancy nipped her chin between her finger and thumb, and knitted her brows till her eyebrows appeared to meet. "I saw it this morning. It was lying on a shelf, near a window. I can see it before me now." She waved her hand in the air. "Like a picture. Distinctly!"

"Yes—yes—yes! But where? *Think*! In the big classroom?"

"No–o; I think not. No; certainly not the big classroom?"

"Miss Drake's room, then? The study? Number 5? Our bedroom? If you can see it distinctly, you *must* know."

Nancy frowned on, apparently plunged in thought, then slowly a flash seemed to irradiate her features.

"I have it!" she cried triumphantly. "It was in the window of the chemist's shop! I saw it as we passed by in walk.—A beautiful black brand-new stylo!"

The audience sniggered with enjoyment, for though not quite so heartless as their brothers, it cannot be denied that most school-girls take a mischievous delight in teasing their companions. Dreda Saxon was, moreover, from this point of view an amusing victim, for when a joke was directed against herself her sense of humour was temporarily eclipsed, and she took refuge in what was laughingly dubbed "heroics." Now, as usual, her eyes flashed, her chin tilted itself in air, and her voice swelled in deep-toned reproof.

"That is not funny, Nancy—it is *unkind*! To laugh at people who are in trouble is a sign of a mean, unprincipled mind. I am surprised that you condescend to such depths."

A shriek of laughter followed this reproof, and as she marched majestically from the room Dreda caught a glimpse of Nancy beaming and unrepentant, pretending to wring tears out of a dry pocket-handkerchief. In that moment she mentally added three "heads" to the essay on life, and headed them with large capital letters: Misunderstanding. Mockery. Faithless Friends.

During the next week Dreda spent every moment that could be spared from ordinary school-work in working at her essay, alternating between wild elation and depths of despair as her thoughts flowed or flagged. Her home letter was full of the all-absorbing topic, but Rowena's reply was a great surprise—for behold, pessimistic repinings had given place to an outlook which was positively jaunty in tone.

"It's a nice old world, after all," Rowena wrote. "It is stupid to allow oneself to get humped, for sometimes at the very moment when you believe that all is over, the very nicest things are just about to begin. Put that in your essay, and make moral reflections. 'Oft-times in our ignorance we believe ... but looking back over a gap of time we can see—A trivial word, a passing glance, the choice of a road, on such trifles may depend ... Discipline is good for us all, but joy cometh in the morning.' You know the sort of thing. For once I really wish I could write your essay for you. I feel just in the mood to write pages. I've been out riding with Mr Seton and his cousins three times this week, and the exercise is so exhilarating. The cousins are staying at the Manor House—such nice girls! We have taken quite a fancy to one another, and they lend me a mount, so that we can go about together Mr Seton sends you his best wishes for the competition. We talked about it together when we were riding to-day. He is so clever, and has such beautiful thoughts. He is looking forward most awfully to his life, and says it gets better and better all the time. I feel quite ashamed to remember how depressed and discontented I have been, and how irritable with poor old Maud. She can't help it, poor dear, if she *is* stupid; one ought to be patient with her, and satisfied with a peaceful home life! I *am* satisfied now. To-morrow I go to lunch at the Manor House."

"But it was to *me* he offered the mount," was Dreda's comment, not without a touch of offence. Then with a benevolent impulse: "Oh, well, Ro can have it until the holidays, and then he'll take me." Rowena's suggestions as to the essay were too valuable to be ignored, and the fact that they were in exact contradiction of the pessimistic passages on persecution last added, was no hindrance to an author of Etheldreda's ingenuity. She had simply to write, "On the other hand, it may be said," and in came Rowena's reflections as pat as possible. During those next few days her versatile mind seized on everything that she heard, saw, or read, which could by any possibility be turned into material for the essay, until page after page was filled with her big straggling handwriting, and while her companions were still biting their pens in search of inspiration, she was confronted by the task of reducing her masterpiece by at least one-half of its length. And what a task that was!

"Really," she told Susan with a sigh, "cutting down is more difficult than making-up! I read over each bit by itself, and it seems as if I love it more than all the rest put together, and I simply can't *endure* to lose it; but the next bit is the same, and the next, and the next." She rolled her eyes dramatically to the ceiling. "I am like a mother, called upon to sacrifice one of her children. Whichever I choose, it will break my heart! How I wish I could send in two papers, and have two chances!"

Such a proceeding was, of course, out of the question, so with much groaning and lamentation Dreda cut out the quieter passages, reserving the highly coloured flights of fancy which she considered more likely to attract an author of Mr Rawdon's standing. When at last the typed copies of the twelve essays were circulated in the school it was found, as had been expected, that Susan and Dreda had far out-distanced the other competitors, but Susan's most devoted admirers confessed that her production appeared tame and dull when compared with Dreda's sparkling eloquence.

"I don't quite know what she's driving at," Barbara admitted, "but it sounds awfully grand all the same; and dear old Sue's so painfully in earnest! We'd better resign ourselves to the worst, for Dreda's bound to get the prize, and lord it over us for the rest of the term. Our lives won't be worth living."

"It's the unexpected that happens in this world. I have a feeling that there will be strange developments about this prize. Wait and see!" said Nancy, darkly.

Chapter Nineteen.

After a week's circulation in the school, the twelve typed essays upon "My life, and what I hope to do with it," were packed up and sent to Mr Rawdon for judgment, and Miss Drake begged her pupils to dismiss the subject from their minds as far as possible.

"Mr Rawdon has promised to attend our prize-giving on December the nineteenth, and will announce the result of the competition himself, so that nothing can be gained by discussing the matter before then. It will be useless to question me, for I shall know he more than yourselves, and we have the serious work of preparing for examinations before us. Give your whole minds to your work, and don't waste time on useless speculation."

"Easier said than done," was Dreda's comment on this exhortation as she walked to the hockey field with Susan after the class was dismissed. "It's easy for The Duck to be calm and cold-blooded; she isn't in it, and doesn't much care how it's decided; but to you and me it means life or death. Susan, tell me exactly how you will feel if my name is read out. Will you hate me with a deadly hatred?"

"Dreda, how can you? As if I could ever hate you—as if such a thing were possible!" Susan was breathless with horror, her brown eyes turned reproachfully upon her friend. "Would you hate me?"

"Yes," returned Dreda calmly; "I should. At that moment my love would change into gall and bitterness. I should hate the very sight of your face. Of course,"—she drew a deep sigh of complacence—"of course, in the end my better nature would prevail, but I'm so emotional, you know—my heart is strung by every breath—like an Aeolian harp.—I could not answer for myself for the first few moments, so keep out of my way, darling, if you get the prize, until I have fought my battle and overcome."

"I hope you will win, Dreda. I expect you will. All the girls think your essay the best. I should be miserable if I won and you were angry," said little Susan in a low, pained voice. But Dreda was too much occupied with a sudden suspicion to notice the pathos of her attitude.

"Do *you* think it the best?" Susan hesitated painfully; her nature was so transparently honest that she could never succeed in disguising her real sentiments.

"I like—bits of it—awfully, Dreda!"

"Like the curate's egg. Thanks. But not all?"

"Not—equally well, dear."

"You think your own is better?" Susan's usually sallow face was flooded with a painful red.

"It sounds horribly conceited to say so, Dreda. I wish you hadn't asked. It's only my own opinion, dear. All the others like yours best. I believe it will win. Honestly I do."

Dreda walked on in silence, her lips compressed, her back very stiff and erect. She deigned no answer until the pavilion was only a few yards distant, and even then her voice had a strained, unnatural tone.

"I think we will not discuss the subject any more. Miss Drake said, if you remember, that she would rather we didn't. We ought to respect her wishes."

"I'm sorry," said Susan meekly. She was not the one who had introduced the subject, but she was quite willing to take the blame upon herself, willing to endure any amount of blame if only Dreda would be kind and love her once more.

For the rest of the term the whole routine of the school was arranged for the benefit of those girls who were going in for the different examinations at Christmas; and those who, like Dreda, had not entered their names were necessarily somewhat left out in the cold. They took part in the same classes, but it was not in teacher-nature to take quite so keen an interest in them as in those whose prowess might add to the reputation of the school. If an ordinary scholar were inclined to "slack," now was her chance to do so with the least chance of discovery or punishment, and it is to be feared that Dreda, among others, did not disdain to do so.

"I disapprove of this modern method of *cram*," she announced in a home letter. "Young girls need rest and amusement, not one long, continual grind; and I don't think it's feminine to be so learned. Accomplishments give far more pleasure, and you ought to be unselfish in life. I should like a new dress for the prize-giving, please. Something very nice—blue—and extra well made, because it may be noticed a good deal. I'm so glad you are all coming. It will be nice for you to see Mr Rawdon. I am looking forward to it fearfully much."

The new dress arrived in due course, and was all that could be desired. Dreda beamed complacently as she fastened the last button and regarded her reflection in the glass at two o'clock on the afternoon of the nineteenth of December; but her satisfaction was somewhat damped by the discovery that her favourite little pearl brooch was missing, making still another of those mysterious disappearances by which she had been annoyed during the whole of the term.

"I really can *not* bear it. It's too much! It would try the patience of Job!" she cried passionately. "Someone is bent on driving me frantic, and whoever she is she's a mean, dastardly wretch. Sometimes,"—her eyes flashed upon Nancy, who sat upon her bed leisurely brushing out her long brown mane—"sometimes, Nancy, I believe it is *You*."

Susan, glancing fearfully across the room, saw Nancy's shoulders give a slight involuntary jerk, but she made no other sign of perturbation, and voice and manner remained as usual, calmly nonchalant.

"*Do* you?" she queried, smiling. "How interesting! And what has led you to that conclusion, may I ask?"

"Your own character. You take a delight in teasing and worrying and mystifying people out of their senses. You probably think it amusing to hide my things, and see me rushing about searching desperately in every corner. I'm good sport, I suppose, because I'm so easily roused. Things affect me more than other people, because I'm so sensitive. I'm like—"

"An Aeolian harp—I know! I've heard the comparison before," said Nancy, with a quiet nod of the head which was infinitely exasperating. Dreda stamped her foot upon the floor.

"Have you hidden my brooch or have you not? Answer me this moment! I have not time to waste."

Nancy rose to her feet and selected a hair ribbon from a drawer with an air of unruffled composure.

"I'm sorry, but I find myself unable to oblige you. If I am the person who has been playing tricks with your things all this time, you can hardly expect me to prove my guilt out of my own mouth. On the other hand, if I am innocent—"

"Well?"

"Then I should naturally be too proud and wounded to vindicate my honour!"

Dreda stood irresolute—swayed one moment towards penitence, the next to anger. From the farther end of the room Susan mutely gesticulated appeals for peace. What would have happened next it is impossible to say, for at that moment a knock sounded at the door, and a voice cried:

"Miss Saxon. Wanted, please! In the drawing-room."

No need to inquire the meaning of that summons! Dreda flew breathlessly downstairs, and in the moment of opening the drawing-room door beheld her four dear visitors standing in the alcove made by a rounded window— father, mother, and two sisters. Such darlings—such darlings; so infinitely more attractive than the other relations with whom the room was full! Father was handsomer than ever, mother so sweet and elegant, Maud was for the moment quite animated, while Rowena in her blue dress and ermine furs was a beauty—so dazzling a beauty, and withal so sweet, and bright, and womanly in expression, that the schoolgirl sister was breathless with admiration. When the first greetings were over and the parents were talking to Miss Drake, Dreda slipped her hand within Rowena's arm, and gave it a rapturous squeeze.

"Ro, you are lovely! Everybody is staring at you, and I'm just bursting with pride... You dear old thing! What have you done with yourself to look so nice? You are fifty times prettier than you were!"

"Oh, Dreda! Am I—am I, really? I'm so glad!" cried Rowena, smiling. But Dreda noticed with amazement that she didn't seem a bit conceited; if such a curious thing could be believed true, there was a hitherto unknown modesty and self-forgetfulness about her manner. "You look a darling yourself," Rowena added affectionately. "Are you going to get a lot of prizes to make us proud of you too?"

"Nary a one," said Dreda with a grimace. "The girls are so horribly clever in this school. I have no chance against them. We Saxons are different; we have the artistic temperament; it's more interesting for daily life, but it doesn't pay in exams. I am simply nowhere in the lists."

"But the essay, dear—the great essay on Life! Surely *there*—"

Dreda bridled, and held up a modest hand.

"Impossible to say. Nobody knows. Mr Rawdon will announce it himself. There he is—over by the fireplace, talking to Miss Drake. Fancy an author looking like that! Quite smart and shaved, like an ordinary man. I expected yards of beard. Oh, dear! my life is in his hands, and he is laughing and talking as if nothing were going to happen! At three o'clock we have all to go down to the big classroom. Sit where you can see me, Ro, and smile at me encouragingly when he gets up; but if someone else wins, look the other way—I shall want to hide my anguish."

Rowena laughed—a trill of merry, irresistible laughter, and the stare of scornful reproach failed to move her to penitence.

"You funny girl—you funny girl! Oh, Dreda, you *do* exaggerate! A passing disappointment like that! Such a little, little thing, when there are such big prizes waiting in life! Oh, Dreda, you are *young*!"

"Oh, Rowena, you are—" The retort hung fire, for at the moment it seemed impossible to think of the right word to express what Rowena was. "*Changed*!" came at last, as a somewhat tame conclusion, but at least it had the effect of making Rowena blush from the tip of her dainty chin to the very roots of her flaxen hair. Now, why should one blush as though one had been detected in a crime at simply being accused of change?

At five minutes to three the pupils left the drawing-room, and took their places ranged at the back of the big classroom. A small platform had been erected at the farther end, on which sat the teachers, with Mr Rawdon in the place of honour, just behind the water-bottle on the table. Parents and friends sat in chairs running sideways down the room, so that they were able to see the girls and watch the progress of happy prize-winners towards the platform. Rowena smiled confidently at her sister, but Dreda had forgotten her sister's existence. Her heart was beating in quick, sickening thuds; her feet and hands were icy cold; her knees jerked up and down, and in her throat was a hard, swelling pain. It seemed as if all the happiness of life depended upon the next few minutes; as if she could never hold up her head again if she failed now. The girls were smiling and nudging each other gaily; Norah was whispering to Susan, and Susan was listening with an air of genuine interest. Were they all sticks and stones, who had no capacity for feeling? Then Mr Rawdon rose to his feet, and there was an outburst of clapping from the audience. Dreda's own hands moved automatically, and again she wondered at their cold. The first few sentences sounded like a meaningless buzz; then gradually her brain took in the words. Mr Rawdon was expressing conventional pleasure at the "privilege" accorded him by his "kind friend;" these formal civilities were just the clearing of the way before the real business began, and speaker and hearers alike heaved a sigh of relief when they were over and the interesting criticism had begun. Mr Rawdon considered that four out of the twelve essays submitted to him were decidedly above the average of such productions, showing evidences of originality, thought, and literary style. His lips twitched humorously as he described himself as having been quite overwhelmed by the flights of eloquence of one of these budding authoresses, but although four essays had stood out conspicuously from the rest, he had not had a moment's hesitation in deciding on the prize-winner. The essay of this young writer bore the inevitable marks of youth and inexperience, but it bore something else too—something which it was a joy to discover—something which had given himself as a writer a deep pleasure and satisfaction—it bore the marks of a strong literary gift. The girl who had written this essay possessed the great gifts of wit, pathos, and charm; she could not only feel, but she could clothe her thoughts in apt, telling words. She had faults to overcome, and her apprenticeship to art might be long and hard; but he had confidence in making a prophecy to-day, a prophecy which he called upon his hearers to remember and recall in after years, a prophecy that the writer of this schoolgirl essay would live to make an honoured name for herself in the English-speaking world.

A wild burst of applause sounded from the benches at the back of the room. Mr Rawdon smiled, and lifted a slip of paper from the table before him.

Chapter Twenty.

Mr Rawdon deliberately fastened his eye glasses on his nose, and looked down at the slip of paper. There was a dead breathless silence in the room.

"The name of the prize-winner is Etheldreda Saxon."

It seemed to Dreda that her very heart stopped beating in that moment of wild, delirious joy. It was almost as though she had received a blow on her head, so dazed and paralysed did she appear; then dimly she was conscious of the sound of clapping and stamping, and looking across the room the four dear familiar faces stood out in bold relief, while all the others remained a mist and blur. Father quite pale, with his eyes shining like blue flames; mother with the tears streaming down her face—why did mothers always cry when they ought to be glad?—Rowena, one sweet, glowing smile of delight. Maud with her mouth wide open—one could almost *hear* her snore.

The clapping went on—everyone seemed to be staring in her direction, and someone was pressing her arm, and saying gently: "Go, dear—go! They are waiting for you. Go for your prize!"

It was Susan's voice. Susan's face was looking at her with the sweetest, kindest smile... With a start Dreda came back to herself, and as she did so half a dozen words sounded in her brain as distinctly as though spoken by a real human voice. "That is love!" said the voice. "That is the true love!" As she walked up the bare centre of the floor she was thinking not of her own triumph, but of Susan's unselfish joy; it came to her mind that Susan's triumph was greater than her own.

Once on the platform, however, face to face with Mr Rawdon, with Miss Drake by his side beaming with happy smiles, conscious of being the cynosure of every eye, it was impossible not to feel a natural pride and elation.

Before presenting the pile of handsomely bound volumes—ten in all—Mr Rawdon held out his hand with a very charming gesture of friendship.

"Etheldreda Saxon, I congratulate you on what you have achieved in the present; I congratulate you still more on what you are going to achieve in the future! My good friend Miss Drake, knowing of old my unmethodical methods, told me not to trouble to return the manuscripts of the various essays submitted for my criticism, but before leaving home to-day I put your typed copy in my pocket, thinking that you would naturally like to have it. I return it to you now, together with these books, which, to my mingled pride and embarrassment, have been chosen for your prize. I hope and expect that the time will come when those present this afternoon may feel *it* one of their happiest recollections that they were present on the occasion when Etheldreda Saxon received her first literary recognition."

Thunderous applause. Dreda walked down the little stairway, carrying her heavy load of books with the folded manuscript slipped beneath the cover of the topmost volume. The visitors on either side beamed congratulations as she passed; on the faces of her school friends was an expression which she had never seen before—proud and *yet* awed, affectionate yet shrinking. It was as if they said to themselves:

"Who is this Dreda who has changed into a genius before our eyes? We have laughed at her, and made fun of her pretensions, and behold, they are not pretensions at all—*they are real*! We have been blind. We have never really known her as she is."

The girls in the second row made way for her as she came, pulling their skirts aside, and tucking their feet beneath the bench to allow her to pass along to her seat. She saw each face quite close as she passed along— Flora, Barbara, Nancy, Norah, Grace—all smiled shyly upon her—all except one. Norah's eyes remained hard and cold—Norah was not glad. She wanted Susan to win the prize.

The clapping was dying down, and Mr Rawdon was beginning his promised address.

"My dear friends—It is my privilege this afternoon—" It was not possible to listen to an address at this supreme moment of realisation—even the words of Mr Rawdon himself were a meaningless jargon in Dreda's ears. Someone tried to take the books from her, but she clung tightly to the volume containing the precious essay which had brought this triumph into her life. Such a wonderful essay that on the strength of it one of the greatest of living authors had confidently prophesied a worldwide reputation. She, Dreda Saxon, an author whom strange people talked about, whose name appeared familiarly in newspapers and magazines! She herself had dreamed of such fairy tales, had expatiated on their probability to sceptical friends; but now that Mr Rawdon had prophesied the same thing she was none the less surprised and tremulous. He who has experienced what the world calls triumph knows well that at those moments the inmost feeling of the heart has been *humility* rather than pride. He alone knows his own limitations, his own weakness; he trembles lest he may prove unworthy of the praise he has won. As the first delirious moments passed by, Dreda was amazed to feel a sense of depression chilling her blood. She questioned herself as to its cause, and discovered that it arose from a new and disagreeable doubt of her own capacities. Mr Rawdon thought her very, very clever; but was she—*was* she really? He believed that she could write books—long books of hundreds of pages, like the one lying on her lap; many books—one after another—all different, about different people, different things. Could she do it? Was her brain really full enough, wise enough, original enough for such a strain? Face to face with herself Dreda experienced some horrible moments of doubt. It had been so difficult to write that one essay—of herself she had seemed to have no ideas. She had merely pounced on what other people had written and said and rearranged their words. "I am quick, I am sharp. I am what they call *ready*," said Dreda to herself in that rare moment of modesty; "but I am not really clever. I don't think thoughts of my very own like Susan. It's all a mistake. I shall fail, and everyone will know."

She began to tremble again, and the form creaked behind her. Some one edged nearer and pressed a supporting arm against her side. It was Susan. *Dear* Susan! If she had been cross and jealous it would have spoiled those first wonderful moments of triumph. Dreda remembered her own prediction of how she would have felt had positions been reversed, and pressed lovingly against the thin little arm. Her eye fell on the sheets of manuscript folded within the book on her lap, and at the sight she knew a returning thrill of confidence. After all Mr Rawdon was a better judge than herself—he would not have spoken as he did if he had not been sure. It was one of the signs of greatness to distrust oneself.

Dreda smiled, and let her fingers touch the paper with caressing touches. She turned back a corner of the sheet and read some scattered words; even in this short time they seemed unfamiliar, and she searched mentally for the context. It refused to be recalled. She lifted another corner, and a third; her hand trembled, she turned a fourth corner; her fingers dropped the paper, and clenched themselves upon her knee, lay there motionless.

At the moment of tension when Dreda had been waiting for Mr Rawdon's announcement, she had felt a strange bursting sensation in her head; but now something really *did* snap—it must have done, for she heard it with her ears—a sharp, splitting noise, so loud that it seemed impossible that others had not heard it also; yet they still sat smiling and complacent. No one knew, no one suspected. They still believed what she herself had believed, a moment ago—long, long years ago—which was it?—that she was the winner of the coveted prize, the clever, fortunate girl who had a future before her, whose name was to be a household word in the land. She had thought so too; she had walked down the room to the sound of applause, had felt every eye riveted on her face, had seen her mother's tears; but this paper which lay on her knee, the paper with "Prize Essay" scrawled across the back—this was not her composition. The sentences which she had read were not her own; there had been some mistake—some horrible, incomprehensible mistake! The numbers must have been confused together. It was Susan's essay which had won the prize, and not her own.

Three minutes ago she had been sure, yet she had not been happy; she had allowed herself to think of the future—to worry and to doubt. Oh, the folly of it! And now she could never be happy any more; her triumph was turned into humiliation and shame.

What would they think—do—say? Mr Rawdon, Miss Drake, father and mother, the other visitors, the girls? What *could* they say? It would be miserable for everybody—even for Susan. Susan could not enjoy her triumph at such a cost to her chosen friend. Susan's arm pressed lovingly against her side—she was distressed that Dreda seemed unnerved, but she did not guess what had happened. Nobody guessed! No one could guess if she kept those sheets carefully folded, and destroyed them as soon as she reached the dormitory. It was not her own mistake. It was Mr Rawdon's. Was one called upon to taste the very dregs of humiliation because another person had made a mistake?

Mr Rawdon was still talking. The hands of the clock had only registered ten minutes since he began; it seemed a lifetime before the big hand reached the next figure. No; she would not tell. The mistake had happened, and she must abide by it. There were other people to think of besides herself. Mother had cried for joy; father's eyes had glowed with happy pride—could they bear to have their joy turned to pain?

133

Mr Rawdon was talking about life, taking up the subject of the girls' essays, enlarging upon what they had tried to express. The words floated to Dreda's ears; she listened in curious, detached fashion. "Difficulties and temptations came to us all; they were hard to bear, bitterly hard at the time, but looked upon in the right light they were just opportunities given to us to prove our true worth, to help us farther on our way." Fine words, fine words! It was easy to preach when all was going well for oneself, and there was no terrible mountain of difficulty blocking up the very next step. She *could* not tell! All the eyes would stare at her again, but the admiration would be changed into pity—perhaps even into suspicion. Some people might believe that she herself was responsible for this mistake. She would give Susan another copy of the books for Christmas. Susan should not suffer. She would not tell.

Mr Rawdon had put down his notes, the hands of the clock had touched yet another figure; he was looking down the room and smiling in her direction. She lost the drift of his sentence, but his last words were her own name—"an Etheldreda Saxon," he said, and in the midst of the applause which followed a girl's voice rang out: "Three cheers for Dreda Saxon!" And once more the room was in an uproar of delight.

The girls leapt to their feet; Dreda leapt with them. Susan felt her thrust her way forward, and stared in surprise. She feared that her friend had turned faint with emotion, but when Dreda had cleared herself from the crowded forms she marched quietly up the room towards the platform. The unfolded essay was in her hand, her face was as white as the paper itself. The applause died away into a tense, uneasy silence. Something had gone wrong. What could it be?

Dreda held up the essay towards Mr Rawdon.

She opened her lips, but it was only after several ineffectual efforts that the husky voice would come.

"It is not mine! There has been a mistake. Susan wrote it—Susan Webster—the prize is hers!"

Chapter Twenty One.

A blank silence followed Dreda's announcement. Dismay, disappointment, and distress seemed printed on every face. Mr Rawdon and Miss Drake gazed first at each other, then at the girl, then at the paper which she had laid upon the table. Their foreheads were fretted with perplexity. For the first few moments they seemed unable to speak; but presently, bending towards Dreda, they appeared to question her in whispered tones, to question anxiously, to cross-question,—to draw her attention to page after page of the typed essay, as if searching for a refutation of her statement. But Dreda shook her head, and could not be shaken. Then Miss Drake turned aside and sat down, turning her chair so that her face was hidden from the audience, and two little patches of red showed themselves on Mr Rawdon's cheek bones.

"Ladies and gentlemen," he began, "a mistake has arisen—a most regrettable mistake. The numbers attached to two of the essays submitted to me have apparently been misplaced. It is impossible to say how this confusion has arisen. Neither Miss Drake nor I can think of any satisfactory explanation. If by chance it should be due to any carelessness of my own, I can only say that I am most deeply sorry, and that I feel myself painfully punished. It appears that the writer of the prize essay is not Etheldreda Saxon, as we believed. She herself discovered the mistake when glancing at the paper which I had returned to her while I was giving my address just now, and has taken the first possible opportunity of making public her discovery. I regret more than I can say that she should have had so painful an experience, and I am sure that you will all share my sorrow. Miss Saxon's essay was one of the four chosen from the rest, and I can only hope that the prophecies which I have already made as to her future will in all truth be fulfilled." (Great applause.) "I now call upon Miss Susan Webster, the author of the selected essay, to come up to the platform and receive her prize." (Faint clapping of hands.)

There is no doubt that it was a painful anticlimax. It is not often that a literary genius looks the part so delightfully as Dreda had done twenty minutes before—Dreda, in her new blue dress, with her flaxen mane floating past her waist, her beautiful eyes darkened with excitement, her complexion of clearest pink and white. As she had mounted the steps to the platform the watching faces had shone with pure artistic pleasure in the sight. So young, so strong, so lovely, and so gifted—it was a privilege even to look upon so fortunate a creature. And now! Guided by Miss Drake's thoughtful hand, the fairy princess had slipped behind the screen which hid the back of the platform, and creeping slowly across the floor came the mouselike figure of Susan in her dun brown dress, her plain little face fretted with embarrassment and distress, a victor with the air of a martyr, a conqueror who shrank from her spoils.

Despite himself, Mr Rawdon's voice took a colder tone as, for the second time, he presented the pile of books; despite herself, Miss Drake's smile was mechanical and forced; while the visitors made only a show of applause. "Hard luck for that fine, bright girl!" whispered the fathers one to another; the mothers almost without exception had tears in their eyes. "And she looks so sweet and pretty! It's a *shame!*" cried the sisters rebelliously. Even the girls on the benches at the back of the room—Susan's companions who loved her and appreciated her worth—even they looked oppressed and discomfited. The romance of Dreda's triumph had appealed to their young imaginations; they understood even more keenly than their elders the suffering involved in that humiliating confession. "Poor Dreda!" they whispered to each other. "Oh! poor old Dreda!"

At tea in the drawing-room the tone of the teachers was distinctly apologetic—the high spirits characteristic of the early hours had ebbed away, and the visitors were glad to beat an early retreat. Mr and Mrs Saxon received Miss Drake's apologies in the kindest and most sympathetic manner, and would not allow her to take any blame to herself.

"It was an accident—no one can be blamed. We are so sorry for you, too!" Mrs Saxon said sweetly. "It is a disappointment, of course; it was a very happy moment when we believed our dear girl had gained such a prize. We were so proud of her!"

"We are proud of her now," interrupted Dreda's father quickly, and at that both his hearers smiled and nodded their heads in sympathetic understanding. "Yes, yes; we are proud of her *now.*"

To Dreda herself her parents made no allusion to the tragic mistake. The girl only made her appearance when the motor drove up to the door, and her cool, somewhat haughty manner showed that sympathy was the last thing which she desired at the moment.

"Good-bye, darling, till Thursday. Only two days more before we have you back among us."

"Good-bye, my girl. I'll drive over for you on Thursday morning."

"Dreda, darling, I'm so glad you are coming. I've such lots to tell you!"

"You've got your belt fastened on the wrong hook. The point's crooked."

For once Maud's literal mind was a blessed relief. Her parting words made everyone laugh, and the car drove off with the cheery sound of that laughter ringing in the air, and the remembrance of merry faces to cheer Dreda's aching heart. She turned and crept upstairs to the study. She had shed her own gala dress, thrusting it away in the cupboard as if she never wished to behold it again. The study was filled with odd pieces of furniture which had been taken out of the big classrooms, and the fire was dying out upon the grate.

"Here sit I, and my broken heart!" sighed Dreda dramatically, as she subsided into a chair and drew her shoulders together in an involuntary shiver. It had been cold work standing at the door watching the departure of the car, and the atmosphere of the deserted room was not calculated to cheer her spirits. "When you've had a great shock your constitution is enfeebled; when you're enfeebled, you are sensitive to chills; a chill on an enfeebled constitution is generally fatal. Perhaps I've received my death blow this afternoon in more ways than one." Dreda sniffed and shivered miserably once more. The stream of visitors was still departing, saying good-bye to Miss Bretherton and the teachers in the drawing-room and making their way to the door. Dreda would not risk leaving the study and encountering strange faces on the staircase; besides which, it did not seem her place to seek her companions at this moment. It was her companions who should seek *her*.

"In the hour of my triumph they all crowded round me; now I am a pelican on the housetop, and no one cares if I am dead or alive. I must get accustomed to it, I suppose. Shame and humiliation must henceforth be my portion. Only fifteen and a half—in *years*. In suffering I'm an old, old woman! Mr Rawdon was sorry; I saw it in his face; but he liked Susan's best. Susan has won the prize. Where is Susan now? Has she forgotten all about me?"

As if in answer to this question the handle of the door turned, and a head was thrust round the corner. A voice exclaimed: "Here she is!" and Nancy entered the room, followed closely by Susan herself. They stood and looked at Dreda, and Dreda looked at them, but none of the three uttered a word. Then suddenly Susan whispered something in Nancy's ear, and while that young person hurried from the room with a most unusual celerity, Susan dropped quietly on her knees beside the dying fire and began coaxing it into a blaze.

Dreda sat back in her chair and watched the process with a dull, detached curiosity. Susan's back looked so narrow and small; the brown dress fastened at the back with a row of ugly bone buttons; as she knelt the soles of her new slippers seemed to fill up the entire foreground. They were startlingly, shockingly white! As she bent from side to side blowing skilfully upon the struggling flames, one could catch a glimpse of her profile, white and wan, with red circles round the eyes. Such a poor, weary little conqueror, on her knees striving to serve her fallen rival. Something stirred in Dreda's heart; the ice melted, she cleared her throat, and addressed her friend by name.

"Susan!"

Susan sat back on her heels, lifting scared, pitiful eyes.

"Susan," said Dreda regally, "I don't hate you. You needn't be frightened. I don't hate you a bit—I'm *sorry* for you. This should have been your triumph, and I have spoiled it. It's very hard on you too, Susan!"

"Oh, Dreda!" gasped Susan breathlessly. "Dreda, you're *magnificent!*" She was wan and white no longer; her eyes blazed. No one seeing Susan at that moment could possibly have called her plain; the lovely soul of her shone through the flesh, working its transformation, even as the leaping flames were now turning the dull hearth into a thing of beauty and life.

Still on her knees, Susan crawled across the few intervening yards of floor, and rested her head against Dreda's knee.

"I'd have given it up a hundred times - a thousand over, Dreda, rather than let you have this experience!" she said brokenly. And Dreda knew that she spoke the truth.

138

It was in this attitude that Nancy discovered the two girls when she entered the room a few minutes later, bearing in her hands a temptingly spread tea-tray. One glance of the red-brown eyes testified to her satisfaction at such eloquent signs of peace, but manner and speech disdained sentiment.

"Corn in Egypt!" she cried cheerfully. "The Duck fairly showered dainties upon me—scones, sandwiches, cakes, *and* a fresh pot of tea. Let's fall to at once. I am fainting with hunger."

She placed three chairs round the table, seated herself in front of the tray, and, pouring out three cups of tea, handed them round with hospitable zeal. Dreda ate and drank and felt comforted, in spite of herself. It was wonderful how the mere creature comforts of warmth and food seemed to soothe the pain at her heart. She even began to feel a faint enjoyment in the dramatic element of her position, to realise that if she had failed she had failed in a noticeable, even in a tragic, fashion. To Susan belonged the glory, yet she, the beaten one, remained unquestionably the heroine of the day!

By the time that second cups of tea had been handed round, and an attack made upon the iced cake, Dreda was ready and eager to discuss her trouble.

"How *could* those numbers have been altered, Susan? Mine was five and yours was ten. They aren't in the least alike!"

"Dreda, I don't know—I can't *think*! If they had come loose and Mr Rawdon had clipped them on again, he would have remembered doing it. At least, an ordinary person would; but he is a genius. Perhaps geniuses are different."

"*You* are a genius, Susan. You ought to know!" said Dreda, whereat the poor little genius flushed miserably, and Nancy, rattling the tea-tray, rushed hastily into the breach.

"Accidents *will* happen! It's no earthly use worrying your head about the how and the why. There it is, and you've got to make the best of it, and forget it as soon as possible."

Dreda rolled tragic eyes to the ceiling.

"I shall never forget. You can't reach the height of your ambition and then see your treasure crumble to pieces in your hands in less than ten minutes, and fall down into a very pit of humiliation without wearing a mark for life."

"Don't say humiliation, Dreda," cried Susan tremulously. "Don't, dear; I can't bear it. It was dreadful for you; but there was no humiliation. There was nothing—nothing of which you could be ashamed. Your essay was very good, too; it has been mentioned as one of the best."

But Dreda was not in the mood to accept comfort. She was miserable, and she intended to be miserable in a thorough, systematic fashion, so that for the moment alleviations seemed rather to irritate than to cheer—

"My essay was only one of the best four. That's nothing. Except our three selves and Barbara Morton, there's not another girl in the school who can write a decent essay to save her life. The others were all as dull and stupid as could be. You have seen them, and know that that's true. If mine was only the fourth best, that's no praise at all. Mr Rawdon made no special mention of any but yours, except when he—*Oh–h!*" Dreda's voice shrilled with sudden panic; she dropped her cake on to her plate and clasped her hands together, staring before her with wide, startled eyes. "Oh–h! Do you remember? He said that he had been *amused* by one of the four essays. His lips twitched, and he tried not to laugh. Amused at the 'high-flown eloquence.' That was the expression—wasn't it? High-flown eloquence! That means rubbish, of course—bombastic, stupid, exaggerated rubbish! Girls, *that was mine*! I feel it—I know it! Susan, you know it, too. You wouldn't say that it was good, even when I asked you straight out. You were too honest to say 'Yes.' Oh! I am not angry. You needn't look so miserable. It was true, and down at the very, very bottom of my heart I knew it myself. When I thought I had won the prize I was only really happy for a few minutes; after that I grew frightened, for I knew it was a mistake, and that I was not really a genius at all, only a rather sharp-witted girl, a ready girl,"—she gave a dreary little laugh—"who could pick up other people's ideas, and string them together as if they were her own. The girls weren't clever enough to know the real from the sham, but Mr Rawdon knew it at once. He saw how—how—" (she paused, groping in her extensive vocabulary for a word to express her meaning) "how *meretricious* it was! He was—*amused!*"

The last word came with an involuntary quiver of pain, and there was silence round the impromptu tea-table. Dreda saw without surprise that the tears were rolling down Susan's cheeks—it seemed natural that Susan should cry. What did give her a real shock of surprise was to hear a sound of subdued snuffling on her right, and on turning her head to behold the imperturbable Nancy suspiciously red about the eyes and nose.

"Nancy!" she cried involuntarily. "You are crying! I never believed that it was possible that you *could* cry! Why are you crying, Nancy? Is it about—*me*?"

But Nancy only jerked the tea-tray, tossing her head the while in her most nonchalant fashion.

"Can't I cry if I like? Can't I cry for myself? If I don't, no one else will. No one thinks about Me! *I* tried for the prize as well as you, and I've far more right to be disappointed. No one ever said I might be great!"

She tossed her head and frowned and pouted, but Dreda was not deceived by the pretence. At her heart lay a warm feeling of comfort and gratitude. In recalling the incidents of this tragic day, it would always bring a throb of consolation to remember that Nancy, the imperturbable, had shed tears on her behalf!

Chapter Twenty Two.

Home again, and home with quite a festival air about *it* in honour of your return. Flowers in every corner, silver candelabra on the dining-table, favourite dishes for every course, a fire in one's bedroom, chocolates lying ready at every turn—it was all most grateful and soothing! Dreda sunned herself in the atmosphere of tenderness and approval, and though no one referred in words to her disappointment, she knew that it was an underlying thought in every mind, and her sore heart was soothed afresh by each new instance of kindliness and care. The first evening was spent according to good old-fashioned custom, sitting round the schoolroom fire, brothers and sisters together, talking over the events of the term, and comparing exploits and adventures. In the dim firelight Dreda edged close to Gurth's side and slipped her hand through his arm; and, wonder of wonders! instead of pushing her away, Gurth gave it a quick little grip, and leant his broad shoulder against hers in response. The boys were on their best behaviour, amiable and conciliatory, without a hint of the overbearing condescension which was apt to mark the end of the holidays. If there was a blot on the general harmony it was to be found in the air of detachment with which Rowena took part in the conversation. She was perfectly amiable, perfectly sweet, conscientiously interested in the different exploits, yet one and all felt disagreeably conscious that she was no longer one of their number, and that her thoughts were continually straying off on excursions of their own. Dreda remembered the parting promise of "Lots to tell!" and looked forward to hair-brushing confidences later on, but none were forthcoming. Rowena remained loving, preoccupied, and inscrutable.

Alone with Maud, Dreda discussed the change in her sister's manner; but Maud's explanation, though verbose, was hardly enlightening.

"She's nineteen. She'll be twenty on the twenty-first of October next. She's got a train to her last new dress. And then there's teaching me... She orders me about as if she were a hundred, but lately she's grown moony. If I keep quite still and ask no questions she begins staring, and stares and stares and smiles to herself. So silly! But it passes the time. When the clock strikes she gives such a jump! I'm not getting on a bit; but I'm glad, because then I shall go to school. She takes no interest in me. I did the same exercises four times over and she never knew, and when I told mother she said, 'Poor darling!' I thought she meant me, but she meant Rowena. Well, if you grow up, you grow up, but you needn't be silly!"

Three afternoons after Dreda's return home a sharp rat-tat sounded at the door, and Maud, flattening her nose against the window, made one of her characteristic announcements.

"Mr Seton's horse. He's got on his new breeches!"

Dreda gave a glad exclamation.

"Mr Seton! Already! The dear thing! How did he know I was home?"

There was a short, tense pause, while Mrs Saxon and Rowena kept their eyes glued to the ground. A sensitive hearer would have felt that pause significant, but Dreda was too self-engrossed to be sensitive; she never doubted that Guy Seton's object in calling was to welcome herself on her return from school, and her first words informed him of the fact.

"Oh, Mr Seton, it *is* nice of you to come so soon! Have you got the horse yet? It's lovely of you to remember your promise."

"My—my—*what* horse? What promise?"

"The horse for me—my mount! You said you would take me out riding—"

"Oh—er—yes! Did I? Delighted, I'm sure!" stammered Guy Seton awkwardly. He looked bigger and stronger and handsomer than ever, but even Dreda could not delude herself that he looked "delighted" at that moment. There had been an expression of blankest surprise upon his face as she had stepped forward to greet him, as if he had been unprepared for her presence, and he had flushed uncomfortably at being reminded of his promise. Dreda stood looking on somewhat blankly while he greeted the other occupants of the room—Mrs Saxon with punctilious politeness, Maud with a smile and a jest, Rowena in silence with a short grip of the hand. Why did he not speak to Rowena? Were they still at cross purposes as on the occasion of their first meeting? Dreda watched with curious eyes and felt confirmed in her suspicion, for Rowena stitched steadily at her embroidery, and Guy Seton never turned as much as a glance in her direction. It was true that on one occasion when she required her scissors he had pounced upon them as they lay on the table, and handed them to her before she had had time to reach them herself; but instead of forming the beginning of a conversation, as such an action should naturally have done, they both appeared overcome with embarrassment, and ignored each other's presence more persistently than before.

A quarter of an hour passed in a desultory and broken conversation, in which each member of the party seemed to continue his or her own train of thought, with little or no attention to the preceding remarks. As, for example:

Guy Seton: "It's such a ripping day. I thought I could ride over and see how you all were."

Maud: "Mr Morris dropped his spectacles in the stable when he was feeding his new mare. He heard something grind, so he thought she had eaten them by mistake. He sent off for a vet., and he gave her things and charged a guinea, and all the while they were on the dressing-table in his room."

Dreda: "I'm always losing things! There's been a perfect fate against me at school this term. It's not my fault, for I have grown hideously careful, and they all turn up again in time, but it's most wearing for your nerves!"

Mrs Saxon: "I met your mother in the village on Thursday, Mr Seton. I was glad to see her looking so well."

Guy Seton: "This brisk weather braces people up. There's a meet at Newstead Market Square on Monday at eleven. Ought to be a good run."

Maud: "Mr Morris's mare cost eighty pounds. Their coachman told our gardener. He said he thought she was gone for sure when the eyeglasses were missing. They've got a gold rim."

Dreda: "People always lose glasses. Flora Mason wears them at school. She draws most beautifully. She had caricatures of all the mistresses inside an atlas. She put them on the back of Balkan States because no one ever looks at them; but there was an earthquake or something, and The Duck turned them up. As a punishment, she made Flora stand up before all the class and draw a copy of her portrait on the board. Flora kept trying to make it pretty, and she said:—

"'Look at your copy, please, Flora; the nose goes to a point, and is *inches* larger!' Flora was *purple* with embarrassment, and so were we all."

Guy Seton: "I was wondering if you would care to follow with us on Monday, Miss Saxon? We'd take good care of you. My cousin is a very careful rider, and you need not be at all nervous of being led into awkward places. We could turn back as soon as you were tired."

Dreda's gasp of dismay sounded clearly through the room, but Guy Seton was apparently deaf to the sound. Rowena had raised her head from her embroidery, revealing a face of almost startling beauty—cheeks as pink as a wild rose, eyes deeply, darkly blue, lips curving into the sweetest and shyest of smiles.

"Thank you so much. I should love to go. I should not be at all afraid."

"That's settled, then!" cried Mr Seton, and breathed a sigh of relief. The air of restraint which he had worn since entering the room gave place to his usual genial, happy manner. He turned to Dreda, questioned her about her work and games, joked and teased, recalled his own experiences, was everything that was kind and friendly, but never a word did he say about the promised "mount"—not a hint that she also might like to attend the meet! Verily it was a world of grief and disappointment.

Gurth opined that it was a "beastly fag" having no horses, but saw no reason why the younger members of the party should not follow on bicycles. Dreda protested haughtily that if she could not go properly she would not go at all; but when the day of the meet arrived and she saw the little party complacently preparing to start, pride gave way before the thought of a long, dull day alone; she rushed to get ready, and pedalled down the drive looking her old complacent self.

Rowena led the cavalcade on Mr Seton's brown hunter, with her fair locks coiled tightly at the back and her hat pressed down on her forehead. She was not quite so pretty, perhaps, as in ordinary attire, but she looked delightfully trim and business-like, and her young brothers and sisters were proud of her and made favourable comparisons between her and the other lady riders assembled in the square. It was a picturesque sight to see the motley collection of vehicles drawn up by the kerbstones, the riders pacing to and fro, greeting fresh arrivals, who kept trotting in from every direction, the pink coats of the men making welcome touches of colour, and finally the appearance of the hounds themselves, preceded by the huntsmen in their velvet caps and smart white breeches.

A long table was laid out in front of the village inn, on which were set refreshments for those who had driven from a distance. The Saxon quartette strolled up and down, wheeling their bicycles as they went, exchanging greetings with acquaintances, and quizzing the peculiarities of strangers, after the merciless fashion of youth. It was just as they reached the farthest corner of the square, and were about to turn back, that Dreda's glance came into contact with a pair of eyes fixed upon her with a coldly antagonistic gaze with which she was painfully familiar.

Norah! By all that was inexplicable, Norah West herself, standing calmly in the midst of Newstead Market Square, more than a hundred miles distant from her home, to which she had travelled a short week before!

Dreda gazed back in stupefied amazement, and even as she looked a second figure detached itself from the crowd and advanced towards her.

"Dreda! I didn't expect to meet you here. I was going to write!"

"Susan! What is Norah doing with you? Don't tell me you have asked her to *stay!*"

"I didn't—but she *is* here, all the same. Her brother came home ill from school, and the others had all to be sent off at once in case it was something infectious. She telegraphed to know if she might come to us."

"Like her cheek!"

"Oh, Dreda, it was horrid for her, too. Just think if you missed your holidays at home! And she had often invited me there."

"Oh, of course, she adores you, so you enjoy having her company. Don't let me interfere! It's delightful that you are so well entertained. I congratulate you, I'm sure."

Susan's lips quivered. Her face was pinched by the chill wind, which gave increased pathos to her look.

"Dreda, I always tell you the truth; it's horrid of me—but I'm *not* glad! I didn't want her one bit. I thought you and I would be often together, and now that she is here that can't be, I'm afraid. But—poor Norah! None of the girls like her very much; there were so few places she could go to, and just because she isn't—isn't *quite* what one would wish, there is all the more reason why one should be nice to her. You remember what you said yourself."

"What did I say?"

"It wasn't about Norah exactly, but one day we were talking about people we didn't like, and you said the best way was to be perfectly sweet oneself, and to behave always as if we loved them, and expected only good things from them, and so elevate them in spite of themselves. I thought it was such a beautiful idea. I've never forgotten it, and now I'm trying to put *it* into practice."

"Oh–h!" exclaimed Dreda blankly. She herself had forgotten her fine sentiments almost as soon as they were uttered, and was not pleased to be reminded of them at the moment. "Oh–h! Well, if you want to experiment, you must; but I do think it's a little inconsiderate to choose Norah as your subject, and in the Christmas holidays, too! Where do I come in, please? Really, Susan, you are too appallingly inconsiderate!"

Susan smiled her sweet, illuminating little smile.

"I know I am; dear; but be patient with me, please, because I'm disappointed, too, and you'd have done the same yourself if you'd been in my place. You may rage and storm, but you *never* refuse to do a good turn! I'll keep Norah out of your way!"

For this morning at least the promise could not be kept; for, once having joined forces, it was difficult to separate again, and throughout the exciting chase which followed Norah made herself so agreeable that Harold and Gurth pronounced her "a ripping girl, worth a dozen of that mumpy little Susan Webster."

"Now they'll want her asked over on every occasion. We shall be *saturated* with Norah! Miserable wretch that I am! Misfortunes dog my footsteps!" sighed Dreda to herself.

Chapter Twenty Three.

The first three hours of the hunt passed somewhat slowly as the hounds sought in vain for a scent, or "found," only to be rewarded by a short, illusive chase. The waits were so frequent that the riders had little chance of growing fatigued, and the Saxon contingent, being refreshed with pocketed stores of biscuits and chocolate, boldly announced its intention of following to the bitter end.

At last the longed-for baying of excitement sounded from within a spinney which was being drawn, while the field waited in scattered groups to right and left. The next moment the long-looked-for fox dashed swiftly across the meadow, making for the nearest woodland, and, presto! all was excitement and bustle. Led by the huntsmen and hounds, the horsemen went streaming across country in a long, irregular line, leaping lightly across intervening barriers, while the less fortunate riders on wheels were obliged to follow the *détours* of the road.

Dreda felt an almost unbearable impatience as she watched Rowena's graceful figure swaying lightly in her saddle beside Guy Seton in his picturesque pink coat. Hateful to come to a meet if you couldn't come properly! Hateful of Guy Seton to have forgotten his promise! Hateful to follow a mile behind and be out of all the fun. She set her teeth, and decided that she would not condescend to follow meekly in the wake of her companions, but, by taking a short cut in the shape of a ploughed road which led across three meadows, would cut off a corner a good half-mile in length. The path was rough, exceedingly rough—but, granted that it was a trifle dangerous, what else could you expect at a hunt? No sooner thought than done. Dreda deliberately slackened pace until Hereward and Gurth had passed on ahead, then turned in at the opened gate, and after a few minutes' painful wobbling to and fro found a deep rut along which her wheels could make a fairly easy progress. The sound of agitated puffings and pantings from behind made her aware that another rider had been rash enough to follow her lead; but she dared not turn her head to see who it might be. The road grew worse instead of better, and the different ruts seemed to merge together in the most annoying fashion. The bicycle bumped and strained, and only by the most careful steering could be kept upright at all. She was a good and fearless rider, but, to judge from the gasps and groans which sounded from behind, her follower was not equally skilful, and Dreda began to realise a fresh danger in her nearness. She determined to cross to the far side of the road, chose what seemed to be the smoothest passage, and swerved violently to the right. What exactly happened it would be difficult to say, as it is always difficult to account for any accident after the event. It was impossible to decide whether the second rider was too close on Dreda's heels, and so volleyed into her at the first sideways movement or whether Dreda's front wheel struck against a rut, and in so doing blocked the way. The only thing that was certain was that the two machines came violently into contact, and that their respective riders were thrown headlong to the ground.

A moment of stunned surprise, and then Dreda sat up slowly; very red, very angry, conscious of a sore elbow, a dusty skirt, and a hat screwed rakishly to one side. She was convinced that she had not been to blame, and that her downfall was absolutely and entirely the fault of that stupid other person who had followed too quickly behind; but on the point of declaiming reproaches, she was suddenly silenced by two startling discoveries: first, that the other person was none other than Norah West, and secondly, that she was lying very still, with her head falling limply to one side.

Dreda felt a sudden chilling of the blood. Her heart pounded against her side, and an inner voice cried in her ear: "Norah is dead! You were saying horrid things about her an hour ago, and now she is dead. You led the way along this dangerous path, and she followed and got killed, and it is *your* fault! Norah is dead, and it is you who have killed her!"

She crawled forward on hands and knees, and peered fearfully at the still face. The spectacles had fallen off Norah's nose. The freckles looked browner than ever against the pallor of the skin. Her face looked pinched and wan, but she was not dead: the breath came faintly from between the parted lips, the cheeks were warm to the touch. Dreda gave a great sigh of relief, and seating herself in the middle of the road, lifted Norah's head with her strong young arms until it lay pillowed on her knee. She searched for her handkerchief, wiped the dust from the unconscious face, and stroked back the heavy hair, crooning over her the while in tones of fondest affection.

"Norah! Norah dear! Norah, wake up! I'm here. Dreda's with you, dear!"

Hitherto Dreda had felt no affection for Norah West; there had been little sympathy between them, and the rivalry for Susan's favour had been a constant cause of friction; but at this moment it seemed the most important thing in life that Norah should open her eyes and speak once more.

In the silent tension of those waiting moments Dreda had a flash of rare insight into the feelings of another. Poor old Norah! She had been snappy at times, but what wonder! It must have been hateful to have a new girl come to school and become the chosen chum of the girl you wanted for yourself; to see her take the lead, while you remained in your insignificant corner. Norah was neither pretty, clever, nor amusing; she was not popular in the school; but, indeed, she had never striven after popularity. The one thing she had desired above all others was Susan's friendship, and that she had failed to gain. Dreda had been accustomed to jeer at the limitations of others; but now, for the first time in her life, she felt a pang of whole-hearted sympathy towards the girl who was so much less fortunate than herself. "It's no credit to me that I'm pretty, but I should have hated to be plain. It would have warped my disposition to look in the glass every day and see nothing but freckles and glittering gold specs. Perhaps it warped Norah's. I ought to have been sorry, instead of proud and superior. And I'm not clever, either—I thought I was—and it was dreadful finding out. I expect she hated it, too. Norah! Oh, Norah, I have behaved like a blind, self-satisfied bat. If you go and die now I shall be miserable all my life—bowed down with remorse! Oh, Norah, do, *do* open your eyes!"

But Norah lay quiet and unresponsive. Where and how had she been injured? There was no sign of blood, no cut or bruise on the still white face. Dreda gently moved each arm, but still without awakening any sign of consciousness. Then, leaning forward, she tried to straighten out the twisted legs. Instantly there came a flinch and a groan, the heavy lids rolled upward, and two startled eyes searched her face.

"What is it? Where am I? What has happened? Oh—the pain! the pain!"

"You are quite safe, dear. You fell from your bicycle. I am afraid you have hurt your leg; but I'm here. I'll take care of you. You know me, don't you? You know Dreda Saxon?"

150

Norah gave a moan of acquiescence. The consciousness of Dreda's near neighbourhood did not appear to be especially soothing, for she turned her head restlessly from side to side, and tried to lift herself on her elbow. The effort failed, and she was obliged to lie back in the same position, pillowed against Dreda's knee, shivering with mingled cold and pain.

"My leg! I can't move it. Don't move! Don't shake me! The least movement is torture. Oh! how shall I ever get home?"

The same thought was beginning to agitate Dreda's mind. Far off, over the distant fences, the heads of a few riders could be seen bobbing away out of sight, as the field swept across the sloping meadows. As well call to the trees themselves as seek to attract their attention! The cross road was too rough and muddy to be much used in winter; it was quite possible that not a soul might pass by for the rest of the day. Dreda shivered at the thought of the long hours of the afternoon during which Norah might be obliged to lie—cold, cramped, suffering, waiting for the help which never came; of the horror of darkness falling over the land.

"I must go for help. There are some farmhouses about half a mile away. I could get men to carry you back. Could you let me lift you—very, very gently—and lay you down on the bank?"

But Norah was terrified to face the slightest movement. So long as she lay perfectly still, hardly daring to breathe, the pain was bearable; but the moment that she attempted to stir such a darting torture seized her in its grip that she was ready to face any waiting, any darkness, rather than allow herself to be moved. She gripped Dreda's hand and the tears welled up in her eyes.

"No, no! You mustn't! You mustn't! I should go mad. Let me lie still. Some one will come. If they don't, let me just die quietly here. Don't move! *Don't* shake me! I can't bear it. I shall die straight off."

There seemed nothing to be done but to soothe and sympathise, sitting as still as possible, stroking Norah's hair, and striving to shield her from the biting wind. The short-sighted eyes looked quite different bereft of their glittering glasses. The aggressive expression had given place to one of pitiful appeal. Norah had never before experienced severe physical pain; it seemed to her like some savage monster lying in wait to grip her with its

151

claws. She lay with her eyes strained on Dreda's face, feeling herself in Dreda's power, terrified lest Dreda should fail her in her need.

"Dreda, am I heavy? Does it tire you to hold me? I've read that people get cramped sitting in one position—that it hurts like a real pain. Oh, Dreda, but it can't be like my pain! Something terrible has happened to my leg. It is broken—or fractured. You can't imagine how it feels. The least movement seems to stab through my whole body. Even if you *do* get cramped, Dreda, will you promise me to sit still—not to move or shake me until some one comes?"

Dreda hesitated miserably.

"I'll try, Norah. I *will* try! I can't bear to say no when you ask me, but I feel as if it were wrong to promise. It *can't* be good for you to *lie* here in the cold and the damp. And you ought to see a doctor at once. You will have to be moved some time, and it is bound to hurt. Couldn't you make up your mind and be very, very brave, and let me put you down and run for help *now*? Indeed, indeed it would be best!"

But poor Norah did not feel at all brave. She shuddered and cried, and clutched Dreda tight with her trembling hands, so that it seemed impossible to deny her request.

The time seemed terribly slow, the wind grew colder and colder, and a thin grey mist began to spread over the meadows. Dreda turned up the collar of her coat, but even that slight movement brought a groan of pain from Norah's lips and a piteous plea to keep still. She set her teeth hard in the effort to refrain from trembling. Her feet were alternately numb and tingling with "pins and needles," but still no sign of a living creature could be seen. After an hour had passed by Dreda was almost more miserable than Norah, who had passed into a dull stupor from which she was aroused only by occasional darting pains. She lay with closed eyes, refusing to speak, but clutching with both hands at Dreda's dress as if even in her semi-unconsciousness the terror of movement still remained, and the cold mist crept nearer and nearer, shutting out the landscape like a heavy screen. Dreda looked at the little watch strapped round her wrist, and saw that the hands pointed to three o'clock. In these short winter days it was often necessary to ring for lamps before four o'clock—only another hour of daylight, and then! What would happen if no help came within the next

152

hour? Would they have to spend the night together—Norah and she? Out in that lonely path? Would they be found lying cold and stark when at last the searchers came with the morning light?

Dreda was beginning to feel a little dazed herself. Even before the accident had happened she had been feeling somewhat tired and chilled, and the mental and physical sufferings of the past two hours had been severe. Perhaps she had been weak in submitting to Norah's entreaties; perhaps it would have been truer kindness to have inflicted the momentary torture, so as to have gone in search of aid; but be that as it might, the opportunity was past, and whether she wished it or not she was now too cramped to move. Her limbs felt so paralysed that she believed that she would never walk again. But the thought brought with it no regret; she did not care. Nothing mattered any more, except that there was no support against which to lean her weary back. She was so tired, so sleepy; Norah's head was so heavy on her lap. Dreda's eyelids drooped and opened; drooped again and remained closed; her head fell forward on her chest. The grey mist crept nearer and covered her from sight!

Chapter Twenty Four.

Rowena and Guy Seton gave themselves up to the pleasures of the hunt, blissfully forgetful of the young brothers and sisters who were following on wheels; and, indeed, of everything and everyone but just their own two selves. There seemed always to be some incontrovertible reason why they should keep by themselves, a little apart from the rest of the field. Rowena's hunting experiences had been few, and her escort was too anxious about her safety to allow her to try any but the very simplest and smallest of jumps. This excess of precaution necessitated many a détour, but neither of the two seemed anxious to make up for lost time by putting on extra speed to catch up with their friends; and the interest in the pursuit of the fox was of so perfunctory a nature that it often seemed more by chance than by design that they took the right turnings at all!

It was after two o'clock when Rowena was refreshing herself with sandwiches produced from Guy Seton's case during an interval of rest, when the hounds were drawing a spinney, that she cast her eyes to right and left over the scattered field, and remarked carelessly:

"I don't see Dreda! The boys are there, and the Websters and Maud; but I don't see Dreda anywhere—do you?"

Guy Seton cast a cursory glance in the direction indicated.

"She is probably behind a tree or a hedge, hiding from the wind. Miss Dreda strikes me as a young woman who can take remarkably good care of herself. Do take another sandwich! To please me! I'm so afraid you will feel faint."

Evidently Rowena was considered less able to look after herself than her younger sister; for on this, as at every moment of the afternoon, she was guarded, directed, and cared for as though she had been the most helpless and timid of children; and the extraordinary thing about it was that Rowena, who was in reality a most capable and self-confident young woman, made not the slightest objection, but seemed thoroughly to enjoy the experience.

Half an hour later on Gurth took the opportunity of another halt to ride up to Rowena's side with a repetition of her own question.

"I say, Ro—have you seen anything of Dreda? She and Norah West seem to have disappeared altogether. I can't think what's happened to them."

"Perhaps they felt tired, and have gone home. Dreda's all right if she has someone with her," returned Rowena easily, and Gurth accepted the explanation and immediately dismissed the subject from his mind.

Guy Seton was troubled with no fears about the missing girls; but hearing Rowena mention the word "tired," became straightway devoured with anxiety lest the epithet should in any way apply to herself. In vain did she protest with the most radiant and dimpling of smiles. She could no more deny that four hours in the saddle was an unusual exertion than that the weather had taken a change for the worse, and that home lay a good eight miles away. The exhilaration of the moment was such that she felt as if it were impossible ever to be tired again; nevertheless, it was sweet to be cared for, sweet to subject her own will to that of Guy Seton. So the end of the discussion was that the hunt was abandoned, and while the field went gaily chasing after a fresh scent, these two riders turned their horses' heads and jogged slowly in the direction of home.

Suddenly an overpowering feeling of shyness seized upon Rowena. Every moment took her farther away from her companions; the country ahead looked misty and solitary; Guy Seton's eyes were fixed upon her face with an expression at once so wistful and so ardent that it seemed impossible to meet it with her own. In her heart of hearts Rowena knew perfectly well what that look meant; but with the curious inconsistency of her sex the impulse was strong upon her to fly from what she had most longed for and desired. Conversation was the best refuge for the moment, and she plunged hastily into the first subject which presented itself.

"I wonder if we shall find Dreda waiting at home! Poor Dreda, she was so disgusted at having to follow on wheels. She refused point blank to come, as she had not a mount; but at the last moment it seemed too dull to stay at home all by herself. She is such a good horsewoman—far better than I am. Perhaps next meet you will be very, very kind and take her with you?"

Guy Seton's face suddenly assumed an expression of acute anxiety and discomfort.

"Why should I take her? You are not—surely you are not *going away?*"

"Oh, no—oh, no; but it is Dreda's holiday. She would love it so! It would be such a treat."

"And you? Does that mean that you *don't* enjoy it? That you would rather stay at home and let her come in your place?"

Rowena blushed.

"Of course it doesn't. I love it, too; but I wasn't thinking of myself. Dreda thinks—she believes that you made some sort of promise that you would give her a mount, and she is counting upon you to keep it. She would be so disappointed—"

But Guy Seton had forgotten all about his lightly spoken words, and was in no mood to be reminded.

"I think she must be mistaken, don't you know!" he protested easily. "It's always the same thing with youngsters of that age. If one is foolish enough to say a word, they leap to the conclusion that it is a definite arrangement. I've learnt that with my own nephews and nieces. I saw so very little of Miss Dreda before she went off to school that I could hardly have had time to promise."

"I don't think it took very much time. So far as I understand, it was on the afternoon when you first met—"

"The afternoon when I came over to call? I remember nothing whatever about that afternoon except that I saw you, for the first time, and that you were unkind to me, and wouldn't speak."

The blush on Rowena's cheeks flamed up again more rosily than before.

"Don't speak of it, please! It makes me hot and so furious with Maud even now. You are not a girl, so you can't understand; but I was so wretchedly embarrassed, and angry, and ashamed."

"But why? That's what I could not understand! You had been sweet enough, and unselfish enough, and hospitable enough to go to the trouble of putting on a pretty frock—I adore that blue frock—for the benefit of a casual stranger whom you had never even seen. Why should you be ashamed of that? I think it was jolly unselfish. It's such a fag changing one's kit. You ought to have been very complacent and pleased. You *would* have been if you could have changed places with me for a minute, and seen yourself walking into the room. If you knew what I thought—"

He paused, and Rowena, scenting danger, resolved that nothing on earth would make her put the obvious question. The resolution lasted for a whole half-minute, at the end of which time a feeble little voice demanded softly:

"Wh–at did you think?"

"I thought—oh, Rowena! so many, many things! I thought that I had dreamt of you all my life, and had found you at last. I thought you were the loveliest thing in the whole wide world. I wished I had been a better man for your sake! I was so happy to have met you, and so miserable because you were cross. It was such a bad beginning that I was afraid you would always be prejudiced—always dislike me."

Again he paused, and Rowena bent over her horse's head, stroking its mane, keeping her eyes persistently downcast. They traversed another hundred yards before the low, insistent tones again struck on her ear.

"*Do* you, Rowena?"

"Do I—what?"

"Dislike me still?"

"I? Oh, what a question! I never disliked you. I was angry with Maud, and with myself—not with you at all."

"But I want so much more. Don't you know that, Rowena? I tumbled headlong in love with you that very afternoon, and I've gone on tumbling deeper and deeper ever since. Do you care for me a little bit, Rowena? *Could* you care? I'm such a stupid, ordinary sort of fellow. I don't know how I dare ask such a thing of a girl like you—the loveliest, sweetest girl that ever lived—but I just *have* to, and that's the truth! I can't stand the suspense another hour.—If I waited long enough would there be a chance for me in the end? If I were very, very patient!"

A dimple dipped in the lovely curve of Rowena's cheek. She was sure now—quite, quite sure! It was not merely a foolish, girlish imagination. Guy loved her. Guy wanted her for his wife. She had entered into her woman's kingdom, and, womanlike, began instantly to adopt provocative little airs and graces.

"But I—I don't want you to be—to be—"

"To be what? *What* don't you want me to be, Rowena?"

"P–atient!" sighed Rowena, and turned her head with a smile and a glance and a blush which transformed the grey winter landscape into a very Garden of Eden for the man by her side.

Ah, well! it was a blissful half-hour which followed, filled with the inevitable questionings and recollections which every fresh Adam and Eve believe to be their own exclusive property. "What did you think?"

"What did you mean?"

"Why did you say?"

"What was the first—the very first moment when you began to care?" Hand in hand they passed along the country lanes, the reins lying slack on the necks of their tired steeds; hand in hand they turned in at the farther gate of the ploughed roads which lay across the fields, and halfway along its length came suddenly upon the two still, half-conscious figures of Dreda and Norah West.

Chapter Twenty Five.

The alarm was given at the nearest farm, and the two girls conveyed with all speed to The Meads, where a doctor was at once summoned to their aid.

Norah's right knee was found to be badly fractured, from the effects of which she had to face intense pain and discomfort for some days, and a long, dragging convalescence. Given rest and care, however, recovery was only a matter of time, and the onlookers were less anxious about her than the other patient, who was raving with delirium in an adjoining room. Dreda, like many robust people, had been more affected by the deadly chill of those long waiting hours than was her more fragile companion. Perhaps in nursing Norah upon her knee she had screened her friend from the biting wind, which had seemed to cut like knives through her own back. She had been like a figure of ice when she was carried into the house; but before she had been an hour in bed the reaction had set in and she was burning with a fever heat.

The old nursery expression, "hotty-cold," was a true description of that miserable night, when she alternately shuddered and burnt, and when morning came the dread word "pneumonia" was whispered from lip to lip. A hospital nurse was called in to aid Mrs Saxon in the care of the two patients. Rowena took over the housekeeping duties, and went about her work with a smile on her lips and a tear in her eye. Poor, poor darling Dreda! It was pitiful to hear her loud, painful breathing. Rowena's heart stood still at the thought that Dreda's life was in danger—but Guy was coming. Guy would take her in his arms; she would lay her tired head on Guy's broad shoulder, and be comforted. Was it wrong to feel that nothing, nothing in the world could be unbearable while Guy's arms held her close?

Susan hurried over to The Meads whitefaced and trembling, longing to help, to be of use; but Rowena waved aside her offers half-heard. She could do nothing. The house was already too full; another inmate would only be an additional burden. But Susan gently intimated that she was not dreaming of offering her own presence. "I thought perhaps you would let me have Maud. It must be lonely for Maud, and she may be a little in your way. If you would let Maud stay with us for a time I would try to make her happy."

"Oh, you nice Susan! Oh, Susan, how dear of you!" cried Rowena, fervently. "No words can express the relief which it would be to get rid of Maud just now. She doesn't know what to do with herself, and she follows us about all over the house, asking questions from morning till night—millions of questions—and she makes mother cry, and upsets the maids, and drops things with a bang outside Dreda's door when they are trying to make her sleep, and—and,"—the colour rose in Rowena's smooth cheeks—"you can't get away from her. She's always there! It *would* be sweet of you to take her, but I'm afraid you'd be very bored."

"No," said Susan simply, "I couldn't be bored. It's the only way in which I can help Dreda. The more difficult it is the better I shall be pleased."

Rowena looked at her in silence. Little, plain, insignificant Susan Webster, whom an hour ago she had pitied with all her heart. She had no Guy to love her. Considering her unattractive exterior, and the inherent love of men for beauty and charm, it was exceedingly doubtful whether she ever *would* have a Guy. But she understood. She had risen already to a higher conception of love than the bride whose predominating joy was still in being loved—in receiving rather than giving! At that moment Rowena had a flash-like glimpse into the nobility of Susan Webster's nature, and her former disdain turned into admiration and love.

When the first painful days had passed, it cannot be denied that Dreda thoroughly enjoyed her position of invalid, with all the petting and consideration which it involved. She was inclined to pose as a heroine, moreover; for had not her own sufferings been the result of standing by a companion in distress! "I could not leave her," she announced to the doctor when he cross-questioned her concerning the events of the fateful afternoon. "She shrieked every time I made the least movement. It was the knee that was broken, but the pain seemed to stretch all the way up. It would have been cruel to move her."

"One has sometimes to be cruel to be kind, Miss Dreda. It would have been better for her, as well as for yourself, if you had insisted upon going for help at once," said the doctor in reply; but even as he spoke he laid his hand on her shoulder with a friendly pat, and Dreda felt complacently convinced that he considered her a marvel of bravery and self-sacrifice.

Mrs Saxon was the most devoted of nurses, and shed tears of thankfulness over each step of the invalid's progress towards convalescence; but Dreda was by no means satisfied with the attitude of her elder sister. Rowena floated in and out of the sick-room with a smile and a kiss; but instead of begging to be allowed to stay, she seemed always in a hurry to be gone, and on one or two occasions when Dreda made feeble efforts at conversation, her attention wandered so hopelessly that she said "Yes" and "No" in the wrong places, or blushingly requested to have the question repeated.

"How odd Rowena is! So absent-minded and stupid. She doesn't listen to half one is saying, and smiles to herself in the silliest way.—I think the housekeeping must be too much for her brain!" Dreda declared to her mother, and Mrs Saxon smiled in response and skilfully turned the conversation to a safer topic. Dreda was not strong enough to bear any excitement yet awhile.

It was nearly a week later, when one morning, as Rowena stood by the bedside, the invalid's quick eyes caught the flash of diamonds on the third finger of her sister's left hand. She pounced upon it, and holding it fast, despite the other's struggles, demanded tersely:

"What's that?"

"Oh, Dreda, I—I have been waiting to tell you! The doctor said you were to be kept so quiet. It's a—a— Guy gave it to me."

"Guy?" The face on the pillow was all blank surprise and bewilderment. "What Guy?"

"Guy Seton—my Guy! It's an engagement ring. Oh, Dreda, I have been longing to tell you. I'm so—happy!"

"You—are—engaged—to Guy Seton?" repeated Dreda blankly. Instead of the radiant smile which Rowena expected, her face hardened with displeasure, and she drew her brows together in a frown. "When? How? Why? I never dreamt of such a thing. It seems too extraordinary to be true."

"Oh, Dreda, why? We think it so natural. We were made for each other. It seems as if we must always have been engaged. I thought you would be so pleased."

"Well, I'm not," declared Dreda decidedly. "Not at all. I don't like it one bit. It upsets all my plans. I used to imagine that father would get all his money back and I should come home from school and go about with you—two fair young *débutantes*—always together, having such fun, sitting up afterwards in our bedrooms brushing our hair and talking over what had happened as they do in books. It will be so dull being alone with no one but Maud. Oh, Rowena, you *are* selfish!"

But Rowena only laughed, and dimpled complacently.

"Oh, Dreda, you *are* funny! You didn't expect me always to stay at home, did you? I am the eldest; it is only natural that I should be married first, and if I *am* to be married, surely you would rather have Guy than anyone else! There is no one like him. All the men we have known are like puppets compared with him. He is so true, so strong, so noble. You ought to be proud, Dreda, that you are going to have him for a brother."

"Well, I'm not," declared Dreda once more. "It's not a bit what I expected. I thought that first day he seemed so taken with *me*! I thought—at least, I didn't think, but I *should* have thought if I had thought, do you understand?—that he would have wanted to be engaged to *me*! Not yet, of course, but he could have waited till I was grown up. And you were so huffy and stiff, and I raced across the fields to find mother, and took such trouble. It doesn't seem fair!"

But Rowena only laughed again, without a trace of offence.

"Poor old Dreda, it *is* hard lines. Never mind, dear; think of the wedding, and how you will enjoy being chief bridesmaid, and how lovely it will be when you come to stay with me in my own little house. Won't it be fun doing just as we like, and ordering the dinners, and having parties whenever we like, and being absolutely and entirely our own mistresses, with no one to say: 'Don't!' or 'You must not,' or 'I'll leave it to you, dear—but you know my wishes!' That's the worst of all, for it seems to put you on your honour, and then you're powerless. You must often come to stay with us, Dreda dear."

Dreda lay silently, considering the situation. The prospect painted by Rowena was sufficiently enticing to mitigate her first displeasure. Pictures of bridal processions passed before her eyes; pictures of a charmingly artistic little house, which would be as a second home, an ideal home free from discipline and authority. The frown faded, her lips relaxed, a dimple dipped in her cheek.

"You must let me choose the bridesmaids' dresses, and help to arrange the drawing-room. I should have it green, with white paint; but you must be awfully particular about the shade. I've got a wonderful eye for colour— Fraulein says so. So *that* was why you never listened when people spoke to you, and kept on smiling in that silly way! I asked mother, but she put me off. Rowena, tell me. What did he say?"

"*Dreda!*"

Rowena, drawing herself up with a most grown-up access of hauteur, gave it to be understood that such questions were an outrage on good taste, and her younger sister was obliged to turn to subjects less embarrassing and intimate.

"Well, how did you feel then, when it was all settled and you had time to think?"

"Very happy—utterly happy and contented. There seemed nothing I could wish altered; except, oh, Dreda, I was sorry about the past. I wanted to tell you about that, so that you might be warned in time. Father and mother were so sweet to Guy and me; they never seemed to think of themselves, but only of our happiness; but when I said good-night I saw the tears in mother's eyes, and I said to myself, 'You had the chance of helping her when she was in trouble and of showing her what a comfort a daughter could be; but you were cross and selfish, and threw *it* aside, and now *it* is too late. It can never, never come back. You have missed your chance.' That thought was like a cloud over my happiness. I had felt so disappointed to miss my season in London, so angry at having to teach Maud, so ill-used at being shut up in the country, that I had no time to be sorry for anyone but myself. I made things *worse* for mother by moping and looking cross and dull, and I was a Tartar to Maud. Poor old Maud! She was far more patient with me than I was with her; and after all, Dreda, it was here, in the place I hated, living the life I dreaded, that I met Guy, the big, big prize of my life! I feel so much older since I was engaged. One seems to *understand*everything so differently. And I have thought of you so often, dear, and hoped that you may never lose your chance as I have done mine. Your*home* chance, I mean—the chance of being a real good daughter to father and mother. Then you can never reproach yourself as I do now."

Dreda stared with big, surprised eyes. Well might Rowena say that she was changed! It might have been mother herself who was speaking. Such gravity, such penitence, such humility, were new indeed from the lips of the erstwhile proud and complacent young beauty! Dreda lay awake that night pondering over the great news of the day, with all its consequences to Rowena and herself.

Meanwhile Norah lay helpless in her bedroom at the other side of the house, and though the agonising pain of the first few days was mercifully a thing of the past, the doctor did not disguise the fact that a long and weary convalescence lay ahead before anything like walking could be possible. In a week or two she might be able to be lifted from bed, with the splints still firmly in position; in a week or two more she might get about on crutches, but for how long the crutches would be necessary it was impossible to say. Only one thing was certain: there was no chance of returning to school!

Norah took the verdict very quietly. Once relieved from pain, she was a patient, uncomplaining invalid, and gave little trouble to her nurses. That she was depressed in spirits seemed only natural under the circumstances. Her brother's illness made it impossible for her own mother to be near her; her constrained position made it difficult to read; and her own thoughts were not too cheerful companions for the long, dragging hours. Everyone rejoiced when at last Dreda was well enough to be wrapped in a dressing-gown and escorted across the landing to have tea in Norah's room. A bright fire burned on the hearth; a little table, spread with tempting fare, stood by the bed; and Dreda, propped up in a big armchair, was left to play the part of mistress of the ceremonies.

"They will be happier without us. We will leave them to have their talk alone," whispered the elders to each other, as they left the room; but the two girls were mutually suffering from a sense of embarrassment which made conversation difficult to begin.

"How thin she is! Her nose is sharper than ever. Poor dear, she *is* plain!" reflected Dreda, candid and clear-sighted.

"How thin she is! All her colour has gone, but she looks pretty still. She always does look pretty," reflected Norah in her turn. She lifted her cup in a trembling hand, looking wistfully at her companion with gaunt, spectacled eyes.

"I am so sorry you were ill... It was all my fault. I kept you there in the cold... Doctor Reed says I should have been plucky and made up my mind to bear the pain ... It's easy to talk when your bones are whole. When they are broken and sticking into your flesh you feel quite different. It seemed easier to die than to move, but it was hard lines on you... I'm sorry you were ill."

Dreda beamed reassurement, thoroughly enjoying the position of receiving apologies.

"My dear, don't mention it. I have suffered too, and I *quite* understand. Pneumonia's hateful! I never could have imagined that it was possible to feel so ill. I couldn't have thought of anyone in the world, but just how to draw the next breath.—It *is* so nice to feel well again; but I'm dreadfully sympathetic about your knee. When you were lying with your head on my knee that afternoon, I was sorry I'd been so disagreeable at school. You feel such *remorse* when you've snapped at people, and then see them all white and still, with their eyes turned up.—I thought such lots of thoughts that afternoon, and I'm going to be quite different at school. Much nicer—you see if I'm not!"

Nora shook her head, and her eyes sank in painful discomfiture.

"No! I shan't see. I shan't be there. The doctor says I shall not be fit for school. I shall never go back to West End. Perhaps it's just as well. The girls never liked me very much, and now it would be worse than ever—and Miss Drake—Miss Drake would be furious! ... I never meant to tell, but I've been miserable ever since, and now I've broken my knee—and, when I lay awake crying with pain those first awful nights I made up my mind to tell, whether it was found out or not. It's awful to have a pain in your body and in your mind as well. Did you guess it was me, Dreda?"

165

"You—*what*?" queried Dreda vacantly. Then the colour rushed into her face, and half a dozen questions tripped together on her tongue. "Oh–h, was it *you* who hid my things? All the things I lost? My pencils, my books, my gloves, the clock that I heard ticking in my hat-box, my slippers that were on the top of the wardrobe? Oh, Norah, *why*? What made you do it? Was it for fun?"

Norah shook her head.

"Oh, no. The most deadly earnest. You were Susan's chum, and you patronised me, and gave yourself airs, and I was angry and jealous, and *wanted* to vex you. It was the only thing I could think of, and it amused me to see you fume and rage. I hid them all—every single thing. So now you know!"

Dreda sat open-mouthed and aghast. What she felt was not so much horror at thought of the deliberate unkindness, as sheer bewilderment at the discovery that a human being existed who cherished a positive dislike to her irresistible self. She had disliked Norah—that had seemed natural enough—but that Norah should return that dislike was a thought which had not even vaguely suggested itself to her mind. It was as if an earthquake had shaken the foundations of her complacent self-esteem. She had a second vision of herself as a novice coming among old pupils and companions, laying down the law, starting new enterprises, claiming the first place, and with it came also a new insight into Norah's suffering, seeing all that had been denied to herself bequeathed so lavishly to a stranger. Instead of the expected outburst of anger, Norah saw with amazement the big tears rise in Dreda's eyes.

"I'm sorry, Norah! I was very horrid. You took an awful lot of trouble. I lost nothing, after all, so you needn't worry, and they were all quite little things."

"Not all! They weren't all little. The synopsis, for instance; you didn't think *that* little."

"Oh, Norah, did *you* hide it? That *was* cruel! I had worked so hard—had taken such pains. The Duck was so cross! You took it out of my desk, and put it back when I was in the study, just to make me look careless and stupid. Is it really true? I never for one moment believed that anyone had done it on purpose. I can't believe it now."

"It's true, all the same. I did it. I made up my mind to tell you, and I will... I did worse than that... Can you guess what I did?"

They stared at one another across the neglected tea table; stared in silence while one might have counted ten; then Dreda drew a quick, fearful breath.

"No—no, not that! Not the essay—the numbers—the changed numbers! You *could* not have done that! ... Norah, I *couldn't* believe it!"

"But I did, I did! It was all my doing. I didn't mean to, but Miss Drake sent me to her room, and on the desk was the parcel of papers all ready except for the string, and the girls all said yours was the best, and I didn't want you to win. I thought it would make you more conceited and bossy than ever. I wanted Susan to get the prize, so that everyone should see she was cleverer than you; but I was afraid she wouldn't, for all the girls said yours was the best. The numbers were just fastened on with clips. It jumped into my head that it would only take a moment to put your number on Susan's paper, and Susan's on yours. Miss Drake said we were all to keep our own written copies, for Mr Rawdon, like most authors, was very unmethodical and careless, and would probably mislay the papers and never send them back. She wanted to make it as easy for him as possible, because it was doing her a big favour to read them at all; so she was going to tell him just to send the winning number and not to bother about the papers. I changed the numbers, and ran downstairs, and the parcel went off by the next post. I was glad I had done it. You were so certain you were going to win, and so condescending to Susan. I was glad I had done it!"

"I see—I understand. And—and when my name was read out, when I *did* get the prize—how did you feel then, Norah? Were you still glad?"

"Yes," said Norah slowly; "I was still glad. I knew it was Susan's essay, and I knew that *you* knew. I saw you look at the paper and turn white. I thought you were not going to tell. Then I should have got hold of the essay, and told Miss Drake, and you would have been disgraced before all the school."

Norah spoke with dogged resolution; but, for all her show of bravado, her face flushed to a deep brick red, and her eyes sank uneasily to the floor.

167

Dreda, on the contrary, was very white. Any sort of emotion always drove the blood from her face, and the pupils of her eyes had expanded until the whole iris appeared black.

"You were quite right! At first, for the first few moments I thought I *could* not tell. It seemed too dreadful, after all the applause and clapping. I had to struggle hard to be honest, and all the time you were watching me—and waiting! I didn't know that, but it shows how stupid it is to think that one can do wrong and not be found out. Well!"—she drew a long, fluttering breath—"you succeeded, Norah. It was a great success. Susan got the prize, and I was humiliated before everybody, and heartbroken with disappointment. I thought I should really have to commit suicide that night, I felt so bad. It's the biggest trial I have ever known, so you may be quite satisfied. It was a great success."

Norah looked up sharply; but no, there was no sneer on Dreda's lips. The big, sad eyes stared into hers with childlike candour and simplicity. Norah bit her lip, and swallowed nervously.

"I—I'm *not* satisfied!"

"Oh, but why? You have gained all you wanted. It seems a pity that no one should be pleased. Susan wasn't a bit; she was miserable because I was miserable, and all the girls were sorry for me, and were nicer than ever before. There's only you to *be* glad, Norah. It was your plan, and you succeeded. You needn't mind me. I've tasted the dregs. Nothing can ever be so bitter to me again."

Norah made no reply. Her lips were pursed so tightly together that there was nothing to be seen but a thin red line. She glanced furtively from one corner of the room to another; to the floor, to the ceiling, to anywhere but just the spot where Dreda sat, looking at her with those big, mournful eyes. In her many imaginings of the scene she had never pictured such a *dénouement* as this. She had schooled herself to hear furious denunciations, but the pitiful calm of Dreda's grief was ten times more difficult to bear.

Both girls were still weak and unfitted to bear long mental strain. The shaking of the bed testified to the nervous tremblings of Norah's body. Dreda lay back against her cushions, and the weak tears rolled down her cheeks. The scones and cakes lay neglected upon the table, and the tea grew cold in the cups. Each minute seemed like an hour, crowded as it was with thoughts of such intensity as come rarely to careless, happy youth. Norah looked back on her finished schooldays, and acknowledged to her own heart that her want of popularity was the result, not of the prejudice of others but of her own jealous, ungenerous nature. Dreda, looking forward to the future, resolved to be less egotistical, less confident, to consider more tenderly the feelings of her companions. She had made many resolutions before now—too many! And they had known but a short lifetime. But never before had they been born of suffering, and never before had they been strengthened by prayer. This last resolution was made in a very humble and anxious spirit, strangely different from Dreda's former airy complacence.

"Norah," she said slowly at last, "Norah, you have told me the truth, and it must have been awfully difficult. It's your affair and mine, Norah; let's keep it to ourselves. If you were going back to school, it might be your duty to tell; but you are not, and you want all the girls to remember you kindly. I don't see that it would make anyone happier to know. They believe that it was a mistake for which no one was to blame. Let them go on believing it! It will be better for you, and for everyone else. I promise you, Norah, I will never tell."

"Not—not Susan?"

"Oh, never Susan Susan last of all."

"Why last?"

"Because you, like her best, and because she would be so sorry. Susan is so good that it hurts her when people do wrong. I couldn't bear Susan to think badly of me, and neither would you Susan shall never know."

Then for the first time the tears started to Norah's eyes.

"Oh, Dreda, you are generous," she sighed; "you know how to forgive." Then, with a sudden flash of intuition, "Susan will write books. She will be great; but *you*, Dreda, you will live! You will be better than famous—you will be loved!"

When Mrs Saxon entered the room a few minutes later her quick eyes realised at once the mental exhaustion of her two patients, and she escorted her daughter back to her room and tucked her up in bed.

Dreda's fair head rested on the pillow; but her eyes followed her mother's movements about the room with a wistful expression whose appeal could not be denied. Mrs Saxon asked no questions, but with true mother insight she divined the need at the girl's heart, and hastened to fill it.

"Try to sleep, my little girl," she said fondly. "Try to rest. Take care of yourself for my sake. You are more precious to me than ever, since Rowena became engaged. You don't know how many hundreds of times in the last few weeks I have comforted myself by thinking, 'I have Dreda! Thank God for Dreda! When Rowena goes I shall not be lonely. I shall have my other dear big girl.'"

Dreda's face glowed. The dull eyes shone with happiness and expectation.

"Mother," she cried ardently, "I'll never leave you! I'll spend my whole life helping you and father. I'll never, never leave you for the sake of a horrid, strange man."

Mrs Saxon laughed softly.

"Beware of rash promises, dear. I don't ask that. I don't even wish it. When your time comes I hope you may be as fortunate as Rowena. I am a rich woman. I have three daughters. I shall still have Maud at home."

But with all her new-found humility Etheldreda the Ready could not submit to such a comparison.

"Maud!" she cried scornfully. "Maud could never make up for me!"

Milton Keynes UK
Ingram Content Group UK Ltd.
UKHW041822240823
427419UK00004B/222